I0548776

LESSONS
FROM THE
WRECKAGE

Book 1 of the Lessons Saga

Jonathan E. Furneaux

Lessons from the Wreckage

Copyright © 2020 by Jonathan E. Furneaux

Cover illustration by Rachel Smartt © 2020

Independently Published
ISBN: 978-0-6487696-0-6

www.jonathanfurneaux.com

For Wendy.

Prologue

In his first year at the military officer's academy, at the age of sixteen, Prince Du Mon of Mars narrowly escaped being killed by his teacher.

He'd slept in that morning and had to crawl into his tactics lecture through an open window at the rear of the hall. He slid into a seat, which was when he realised that his roommate Jason was beside him, the picture of a perfect student.

"You slept in," Jason whispered smugly, from the corner of his mouth.

"You're a terrible friend. Why didn't you wake me?"

"I did, twice."

At the front of the room, a twitchy lieutenant commander was gesturing at his console. From the console came a scaled projection of fighters that dogged and swirled around two immense capital ships. The larger vessels exchanged countless volleys of missiles.

Prince Du Mon peeked a glance at Jason's tablet. The blonde pilot drummed his fingers lightly on the simple plastic desk on both sides of the tablet, typing copious notes.

Du Mon opened his academy satchel and then closed it again.

"I forgot my tablet," he hissed.

Jason continued to type a sonata of notes, his eyebrows

and lips wrinkled in mock-concentration. Du Mon looked back at the tablet Jason was typing on, and saw a familiar dent on the screen's upper-right hand corner: a dent from when Du Mon's ex-girlfriend had tossed the tablet out of his quarters. He reached out to take the tablet back.

"Just a moment please," Jason said. "This is a very fascinating point."

When the lieutenant commander looked up mid-lecture, Du Mon was practically sitting on Jason's lap. His right arm had Jason in a headlock, and the other was trying to snatch the tablet back from Jason, who was playing *come-and-get-it*.

"Thank you for joining us this morning, Your Highness," the lieutenant commander called. He performed the caricature of a bow. "How noble of you to grace my simple classroom with your presence."

Du Mon, distracted by still trying to pry the device away from Jason, didn't quite catch the edge in the lieutenant commander's voice.

"Apologies Lieutenant Commander, please carry on," he called back.

There was a nervous giggle from somewhere in the classroom as Du Mon finally wrested the tablet away from Jason and returned to his desk.

"Kindly return your classmate's tablet," the teacher spat.

"This is my mine," the prince protested. "Get off my back."

The lieutenant commander turned to Jason, who shrugged. A muscle in the teacher's jaw strummed rhythmically, visible even at the back of the classroom.

"Let's turn our attention from tactics for a moment, class. A small diversion, I promise. I became a teacher at this college after the Kuiper Incident last year. Are you familiar with this engagement? Yes, I can see some of you nodding."

He began to pace back and forth, the destruction of a capital ship frozen and suspended above his head. He kept his hands clasped behind his back militarily, but cadets in the front row noticed the trembling of the hands.

"A group of Earth Eco-Terrorists had supposedly stolen an Earthen military frigate and bombarded us from range. In the middle of a routine mining operation, the light cruiser I was on received critical damage, and then crashed against the very asteroid we were mining—"

Du Mon glanced over the notes that Jason had been taking, and then back at the projection about him. It was his second year taking the tactics subject. He sighed. *I still don't get it.* It was moves and countermoves, but whereas many students could intuitively pinpoint the mistakes historical figures had made, Du Mon was never able to grasp the basics. On the final exam he'd sat, paralysed, by the question: *how did the First Emperor outclass the Earthen fleet in 3014CE?*

His father, the Emperor, had been diligent in making sure that Du Mon and his siblings were thoroughly instructed. *We won't remain royalty,* the Emperor had said countless times over dinner, *if we become complacent. Education is power, and so we must be educated better than the gods.* It had been somewhat of an embarrassment then, for the entire family, when Du Mon was the first child to fail a subject.

Du Mon was expected to practice the ritual of study perfectly from a young age. He looked up from the tablet and realised that the lieutenant commander was still going, his eyes glued on Du Mon.

"—Why am I telling you this? Because one day you might

be in a similar situation that I was. Pinned down on that asteroid, while the enemy taunted us over the radio channels. I saw their lasermen using the floating bodies of my friends as target practice—"

Outside, Du Mon could see the immense habitat dome that trapped him to the surface of Mars. *I'll graduate soon,* he steeled himself, *and then I can travel the Solar System, away from here.* He looked out at the royal palace. Both the palace and this university, where the officer's academy resided, faced each other across a cultivated garden. Surrounding these two marvels were the countless towers, each one architecturally unique, that contained the parks, shops, and residences of civilians. *If I can pass tactics.* He caught the negative thought, just like his tutor had taught him, and tried it again: *I can pass tactics, and I will.*

Du Mon turned his attention away from the window, and noticed a young officer glancing at him while the lieutenant commander droned on. She turned her body to face the lecturer, but kept glancing at the prince whenever she could. She saw him looking in her direction and bit her lip slightly. Du Mon gave a practised grin, and nudged Jason.

"I'm concerned that this new generation is unprepared to face the horrors of that," the lieutenant commander continued. "Many of you have grown up watching theatre shows that depict war. Maybe that's why some of you are here: to be a hero. Perhaps to have your name immortalised like the First Emperor. However, you should know that for every legend that makes it on-stage, there's a thousand battles where the enemy simply has the upper-hand, and they'll pick you and your ship apart while you watch. Do you see this blade I have here?"

He produced a simple dagger, often given in Martian ceremony. He unsheathed it. The blade was a red, reinforced ceramic. Obviously, no one had told the lieutenant commander that you didn't need to sharpen a ceremonial dagger. He held it proudly in two hands, holding it aloft to the class.

"If you are able to hold your wits about you when you witness that sort of atrocity, the Gracious Emperor might bestow such an honour upon you one day as well. It is more precious than the pathetic medals that Earthen soldiers are given. This proves I am a warrior who protected the crown. What terrors will you face in space against our enemies, and are you ready to face that sort of challenge Du Mon?"

Du Mon had been in the middle of mouthing silently mouthing plans to meet the young lady after class, so hearing his name caught him off-guard.

"My apologies," Du Mon said. "I didn't hear the question. If you are telling me to earn a dagger like that one, though, I already have. The old admiral gave me one for my birthday last year."

He'd expected laughter from the room, but there wasn't any. Jason's hand reached over, warning him. A blood vessel popped in the lieutenant commander's eye, painting the white to a burnished red. From this distance, Du Mon could now see the shaking of his hands.

The lieutenant commander let out a war cry deep in his throat and charged at the prince. Du Mon sat stupidly for a moment, before he remembered the blade. He dove out of the window and onto the university lawn as the cadets inside screamed and cowered from the blade. Du Mon had to run to the palace, desperate and undignified, with the lieutenant commander frothing behind him.

It took five minutes for the palace guards to adequately sedate the lieutenant commander and drag him away. He was tried for treason against the crown, and his ceremonial dagger was confiscated. The academy allowed Du Mon to pass that subject, citing that the prince had undergone a traumatic experience.

1

Du Mon watched the lady he loved while she dressed. After eight months in space, he still found her exquisite. Exactly like he'd asked for.

"You're staring at me again," she said with a look over her shoulder. "Don't you need to get dressed as well?"

"My shift starts in five minutes," said Du Mon. "Plenty of time."

"I thought it took a hundred people over an hour to dress you," the lady said sarcastically as she fastened her undergarments.

"Normally, yes," he said, carefully examining the curve where her hips joined her waist. "But that's the beauty of being out here, I get far less scrutiny."

Harmony bent over to step into her trousers, and Du Mon angled his head to get a better look. She was short for a Martian. Equally attractive was the fact that if she was shy about her height, barely six foot, then Harmony certainly didn't show it. She was a welcome change from the other companion women he'd known. Many tried to bow or curtsy. Another lady had tried to clumsily mimic his royal accent to impress him. He found that one particularly irritating. Harmony was different, however. She treated him a man, and not a prince.

"Hurry up stupid," she said, pulling a thin hemp shirt

over her breasts. "You'll be late for your shift."

Reluctantly, Prince Du Mon slipped out of his bed and found his trousers. He kicked them upward with his foot, and they floated gently up to him under the artificial gravity. His shirt, which he'd discarded a few hours earlier, swam gently across the floor, as though pushed and pulled by an invisible current.

His quarters were large for a capital ship. Even larger than the captain's quarters, perhaps. Du Mon pulled his shoes on as Harmony reclined on his bed. She pulled out her tablet from the corner cabinet where she had stowed it earlier.

The prince stood and pulled on his officer's shirt. He'd been granted the rank of lieutenant upon graduation. The insignia felt foreign and wrong.

Du Mon slid the door open a crack and peered out. A matching room was across the walkway. These luxury quarters were usually reserved for ambassadors or diplomats who needed to be ferried around by the *Socrates*. Du Mon stepped outside, turned, and pulled the door shut. He punched the lock command on the console next to the door, and turned around to stare into the thinnest, most terrifying face he knew. Du Mon swore, and bumped his back into the closed door behind him.

Consul Barclay cleared his throat quietly, and frowned his disapproval. "Pull yourself together Prince Du Mon. You're late for your duty." The Consul glanced at Du Mon's door meaningfully. "I hope we aren't being too distracted by the ship's *luxuries*?"

Du Mon pushed past the tutor.

"Hardly, Consul," he said over his shoulder. "I was simply

put into a deep and unshakeable coma after last night's lecture on responsibility."

He hurried along the tall, narrow walkway, towards the bridge nestled in the centre of *Socrates*. The Consul followed him. The politician had developed a constant stoop aboard the confines of the *Socrates*. He was a goliath at nine feet tall, and loomed over any person he spoke to.

"I know when you're distracted, Your Highness." His voice drawled somewhat as he spoke. "You don't feel qualified for this position, and so you've decided to disappoint everyone on purpose, instead of trying your best and making mistakes."

"So, it's true what they say?"

"It depends what they say."

"That you can read minds."

"Utter nonsense. Who told you that?"

"My sisters."

"Well, I have instructed most of your siblings. In fact, I started instructing you once you started speaking. You pick things up. For example, you missed a button on your uniform."

They passed two spacers: uneducated labourers aboard the *Socrates*. The two men threw lazy salutes as they leaned on their steam-mops. One of them locked eyes with the prince, and received a cuff over the head from the consul as compensation.

"Mind your place," the consul said.

"Are you going to follow me all the way to the bridge, Consul?"

"I am simply concerned that you aren't taking your role aboard this vessel too seriously," said the impossibly-thin

Consul.

"To be frank, I don't think anyone aboard this vessel thinks of my role very seriously," the prince replied. "Besides, I'm just here to learn about the life of the average person, like Ju Tin did."

"Your older brother took that task far more seriously," said Consul Barclay with a shake of his head.

Apparently, Du Mon's older brother had chosen to sleep in the barracks with the lower-ranking soldiers. A decision which had been celebrated by their father. *Learn some discipline, like your brother*, the emperor had said.

Du Mon was the fifth son, and seventh-born to the king, and so the throne of Mars would forever elude him. He'd come to accept that, and yet the royal family had still insisted that he learn the art of war from Captain Dav'i.

After a week onboard the vessel, however, it had quickly become apparent that his father hadn't left rigorous instructions for Du Mon's education. Captain Dav'i had quickly palmed him off to the communications team and left the 'instructing' to Commander Plessis.

Du Mon stepped onto the bridge, relieved that Consul Barclay couldn't follow him. The bridge doors slid shut. Captain Dav'i had publicly banned Barclay from stepping onto the bridge, after the consul had quietly critiqued his leadership style.

The young prince sat at his station and received a sharp look from Commander Plessis.

"Late again, I see."

"My apologies Commander," he replied smoothly. "I was held up by the consul on my way over."

"Yes, the *consul* is certainly the problem," she said, just as smoothly. Plessis had a tight-lipped smile whenever she addressed Du Mon. It was a smile which quickly vanished the millisecond she looked away. "Deimos knows how much a member of the council delights at causing others to be unpunctual. Consul Barclay certainly strikes me as a man who relishes in the chaos of a poorly-organised prince."

She's got you there. The commander, however, had already turned her eldritch gaze to the next task at hand. She worked, with stone-faced efficiency. *What a terrifying woman.*

Captain Dav'i stepped onto the bridge then, and Commander Plessis called for attention. In unison the bridge officers stood, saluted the hulking man at the door, then sat down and returned to work. Dav'i moved about the bridge, inspecting the senior ensigns' workstations.

The console in front of Du Mon lit up with a dull blue light. He tapped his ear twice, activating it, and began the arduous task of scanning the radio by ear. This shift he was going through the utility channels: listening to any chatter from mining vessels that the long-range sensors had detected.

The dull, crackling static of space was suddenly punctuated by the loud noise of computers communicating. He dialled back to the frequency and listened again. It was a rising register. He hit the record function on his console, and ran a check on it. Eighteen digital notes that repeated over and over, and then a crash of static again. It wasn't encrypted like a military signal.

The computer came back with a match: *Earth-Lunar Mining Guild*. Du Mon read through the frequency's description, and realised with a sudden sense of horror that reading any further would kill him with boredom. It was a utility frequency for communicating with long-range equipment.

The computer spat out a refined search: the frequency, decoded, was a simple instruction to arm mining explosives. There were also paragraphs of history about the mining guild. Five reports from HQ were attached about the guild's movements and political alignments.

He stifled a yawn, flagged it as unimportant for the computer, and kept scrubbing the frequencies.

2

There was a faint popping sound from far away, and the *Socrates* lurched heavily under the duress of a warhead exploding under the bow.

The ship's spin rapidly decelerated with the sudden impact, and Captain Dav'i felt himself grow several kilos lighter in his command chair. He gripped the armrests, and waited for the ship's computer to fire the spin thrusters again.

"What are the lasermen doing?" he shouted at Plessis.

Her eyes were wide, and her face was aglow in the scarlet warnings and contacts displayed on her console. "They didn't detect the explosives captain," she shouted as another shockwave rocked the vessel. The prince to his left was deadpan, frowning into his own console in disbelief.

Dav'i flicked his console over to show a projection of the capital ship *Socrates* and its surroundings. Ahead of them, the stars winked slightly.

"Commander Plessis, aim the forward lasers ahead and strafe them in a grid-search pattern," he commanded. She relayed the command without looking up. Dav'i concentrated his own console's screen on the heat signatures further out in space.

"Sensors, have you processed who's firing on us?"

Du Mon hadn't stopped frowning at his console, but he

nodded. "The engine trails look Lunar-made, and the radio traffic is in scrambled Earthen," he said.

Approximately ten thousand kilometres away, the four mining frigates responsible for the warheads launched their corvettes towards the *Socrates*.

"Their flying formation isn't Earthen," Plessis called from the red glow beside him. Captain Dav'i glanced at her console, and saw the red swarm of ships that the central computer was projecting for them. The corvettes danced and dogged in a roughly cone-shaped formation: undisciplined, but obviously skilled and acclimatised to deep space.

Du Mon tilted his head and listened carefully to the radio chatter. "They're broadcasting to the open channel. They want us to surrender..." He stopped, eyes widening.

"Spit it out boy."

"...to surrender me, to give up Prince Du Mon to the Earth-Lunar Miner's Guild. The message is on repeat."

"Bloody pirates," Captain Dav'i shouted. He slammed his fist against his command chair. "I'd rather fight another war."

Several dull-orange plumes of death silently ignited a kilometre ahead of them, rocking the ship as it flew through the shock-wave. The flames were just as quickly extinguished by the vacuum of space.

"Ah, they've laid sleeping missiles on our flight path, like landmines," said Plessis with admiration. "There's no heat signature to detect. The sensors treat them like space debris until we're right on top of them."

"Figure out a solution for it, Commander," Dav'i said. "Helm, new heading of 260 degrees horizontal. Face the enemy directly."

The tall, quiet man from the northern colonies named Dimi, turned and nodded.

"Aye captain," he said, and corrected the course.

"Tactical," Dav'i continued. "Divert 20 percent weapon power to the starboard laser batteries, in case they get sick of waiting and want to remotely launch any hidden missiles. Prioritise the forward tubes. Tell our mining frigates to tuck in behind us at—" he glanced at the console "—at 200 mark 40."

Once the message was relayed, their own mining frigates: the *Sullivan* and *Montessori*, would sit behind them.

Dav'i scratched at his white beard stubble while the instructions were carried out. Then he straightened his bushy orange moustache with his thumb and forefinger. Their own mining frigates might not be the target of this particular raid, but no doubt once the *Socrates* was crippled, the Earthen Miners would happily gut the crew aboard and take the vessels to strengthen their own operations.

"Du Mon, ask one of the comms team to listen for any radio frequencies sent out in the direction of our old heading. I want us to record any instructions they're using to activate those warheads, so we don't have this problem again."

The prince leaned over his console and spoke rapidly to a member of the comms team seated in front of him.

"ETA for enemy arrival?" Dav'i asked.

"Four minutes Captain," replied Commander Plessis. "They're slow for corvettes. Probably have a lot of mass."

"How many are bearing down on us?"

"I count twenty of them," she said. "They're two-person corvettes, possibly retro-fitted with missiles, but I doubt it.

They still have their scoops fitted."

"Du Mon, send a repeating broadcast to Earth asking for intervention. Alert them that their citizens have launched a premeditated attack."

"Will do," he said. "The message will be received in 29 minutes, assuming the Miner's don't bombard the radio-waves with junk transmissions to block us."

"It doesn't really matter," sighed Dav'i. "Just a formality. Earth won't do a damned thing, and why would they? They can say they were powerless to help, while they keep enjoying the riches that the miners bring in."

"These private companies keep disrupting things for us too," Plessis added. "That's got to be worth a fortune to Earth."

"Well, it'll be something for the peacemakers to fight over in a few weeks' time," said Dav'i. "Are the missile tubes ready?"

"Yes, Captain."

Dav'i hit the military-cast button, to speak with the officers on board. "We're engaging the Earth-Lunar mining guild in approximately three minutes. Automated lasers should target down any surprise missiles. Missile tubes should focus down the corvettes. Switch to lasers once they are within range of 800m. Radio frequencies are now reserved for emergencies, over."

He sat, thinking for a moment. "Lieutenant Du Mon, launch the fighters to cover our tail. Tell them to hang back and coordinate with laser batteries. I want them ready to provide assistance."

Then came the waiting. Waiting was always the worst part. Dav'i played with his moustache. Dimi hummed an old folk tune. Plessis slowly cracked each knuckle in her right hand. Du Mon wiped his forehead and coughed. He was whispering into his console to one of the fighter pilots.

"The enemy's corvettes are in range of our anti-fighter missiles," Plessis announced suddenly.

"Fire at will," Dav'i commanded.

3

Tam lay in a tube of metal, while the engineer cycled the airlock shut. The tube was long and cylindrical, with a comfortable chair and crash webbing fastened throughout the interior. Above him, an engineer hit the activation switch and keyed the authorisation. The tube hummed, and lights blinked on across the controls.

There was a soft metallic sound as the docking clamps disengaged, and then the *Socrates* was suddenly above Tam as his fighter craft detached from the underside of the capital ship. The *Invigilator Mk-II* fighter craft resembled a missile, with two rotating auxiliary thrusters mounted on either side for manoeuvrability.

"*Socrates*, I'm away," he said into the controls.

"Copy that Fighter 2," said the voice of a young man on the other end. The words were uncertain and strained.

"You doing okay there flight control? Not nervous I hope?" Tam asked, trying to keep the mood light. *Just what I need, a rookie.*

"Um, just a bit nervous up here. First engagement and all that," the voice tried to laugh, but it sounded hollow, and faded quickly.

"Well no need to fret about yourself," Tam said. Leaning over the controls, he switched on the HUD. A cascade of glowing shapes appeared across the glass of the fighter, outlining *Socrates* and the other *Invigilator* fighters as green friendlies. "You're nice and safe up there. In fact, you should really be worried about poor old me out here."

Above his cockpit, *Socrates* slid through space silently: six hundred metres of once-pristine Martian engineering. The underside of the vessel was now charred and cracked. The heat-treated armour plating had buckled from the impact of the mining explosives.

"How does it look out there?" the voice asked.

Tam pushed the throttle forward with a gloved left hand, so that the fighter kept pace with *Socrates*. The *Mk-II* flight sticks were far too sensitive for his liking. A week earlier there had been a heated discussion when Tam decided to corner the rostered technician, and demanded that an old *Mk-I* flight stick be installed. A great deal of quiet cursing had been heard from the technician for the next few days, but now Tam could feel the familiar contours of the flight stick.

"Contact in two minutes," called Fighter 1, Jace the Ace. "Pair-up. Briefing was rushed because we've been caught with our pants down."

There were a few nervous laughs over the comm.

"Main objective is protecting the tail. If the bastards get near the engines or the mining frigates, we're to chase them away. Highest priority is protecting *Socrates's* engines and systems, and providing support in any blind spots that open up. Second priority is defending *Sullivan* and *Montessori*. Contact in one minute."

Tam felt the electricity underneath his skin. There was a landquake in his gut. Reaching over to the controls again, he hit the proximity alert. A soft hum filled the cockpit. Tam pulled his fighter alongside Jace's, holding course below and slightly to starboard. The humming droned a gentle reminder that Jace's fighter was there. It was reassuring.

"How are you going wingman?" Jace asked. The comm light blinked a private purple.

"The new comms chief is a bit nervous, and it's rubbing off," he laughed. "Who's the new guy anyway?"

"An old friend from the academy," Jace said. "Prince Du Mon."

Tam balked at that. "That squeaky voice is the prince?"

"The one and only, Prince Squeaky." Tam could hear the real Jace slip out underneath the wall that was 'Jason Warsche, Squadron Leader'. Tam missed that side of him: the fun Jace from the academy, who could destroy first-year cadets at cards.

Ahead, the viewport showed the inky blackness of space. The sun sat triumphantly on the port, illuminating the *Socrates* and the other fighters. Several glints of metal were launched from the capital ship, out into the vastness of space. The cockpit hummed.

The computer painted twenty red squares on the viewport, indicating the corvettes that were still invisible to his eyes. The squares grew considerably larger each second. They were two centimetres across, now three centimetres. The cabin lights switched red and a loud collision warning shrieked.

"All fighters dive!" Jace commanded, and Tam reacted instinctively.

The stars lurched and tumbled as they all dove down below *Socrates*. "Swarm pattern delta, Flight Pair B are with us," came the instructions. Tam heard two more *Sequester* fighters nestle into their slipstream. They completed their dive and came up again to face *Socrates*. Twelve red squares had successfully shot past the missile barrage, through the space that the fighters had occupied, and were now turning around in a large arc.

"Command advises the enemy is using hit-and-run tactics," came Commander Plessis' voice. "The enemy has deployed construction drones. Tactical data incoming."

On the viewscreen, *Socrates* was suddenly christened in a snow of red dots.

Plessis spoke again. Her voice didn't betray a hint of emotion. "Fighter craft are advised to maintain a distance of 1km while laser batteries clear drones. Target corvettes."

As they shot past the *Socrates* in pursuit of the corvettes, Tam could see the wriggling, arachnid drones that had been launched like bombs from the corvettes. They landed across the surface of the *Socrates*.

Bright blue welding beams lit up the exterior of the ship as the drones began slowly melting through the ship's armour with welding lasers. The surface of *Socrates* shifted and distorted, as invisible lasers shot out from key installations across the surface of the vessel. They began to melt the construction drones down into slag.

Tam had a mental image of someone carefully scraping ants away from their skin with a hot scalpel. They shot past *Socrates*. Past the long, bulbous fission engines that sat at a safe distance from the rest of the ship. The enemy contacts far ahead had noticed them, and began to bob and weave to make a missile lock more difficult.

"Computer?" Tam asked.

There was a pause, and then the soothing voice of the computer filled the cockpit.

"I'm listening," she crooned.

"Calculate the coordinates at the midpoint between the two corvettes in the lead. Where will their trajectory take them in thirty seconds?"

In the distance, the corvettes began to accelerate to top speed again. Tam looked at the targeting information on the HUD and estimated the distance.

"Here you go," the *Socrates* computer offered the calculations up onto his HUD. He keyed the comm to speak to the squadron.

"I have a targeting plan in five seconds," he said.

"Roger," called Jace.

Tam launched two missiles, two seconds apart. They were ejected forcefully from either side of the fighter, and then their solid-fuel propulsion systems engaged. Two trails of hot-gas erupted, and the twin rockets vanished and became green triangles on the HUD, shrinking into the distance.

There was a dull flash ahead. Four more missiles were launched. Two from Jace and a third set from the Fighter 4 behind Tam.

"We'll pass them in ten seconds," called Jace. "Dive and come about on my mark."

The four missiles bobbed and weaved on the HUD. Two of them vanished, but the other two connected with their targets.

"Confirmed hit against four enemy corvettes," came the prince's nervous voice. "Eight more corvettes remaining."

"Mark," came Jace's command, and Tam pushed the flight stick down to its limit in a dive. Above them, the corvettes silently shot past, faster than the eye could track. His flight group came about again, and Jace punched his fighter forward to chase them back towards *Socrates.*

"My missiles didn't connect," complained Fighter 4, Jenna. "There's something wrong with the targeting data."

"They've turned on their scoops," Jace replied. "Anything in front of them is being broken down into molecules. It'd be drinking their fuel like crazy, but they'd be able to detonate any missiles a kilometre ahead of them, and possibly flinch out of the way."

"That's brilliant!" cried Jenna. "How do we compete against that?"

"It's not brilliant," Tam replied evenly. "You're just as likely to roast your buddies if they flinch into the scoop's cone-of-effect."

"Is that what happens when you speak to Lieutenant Mith?" Jenna asked innocently. "Your brain gets roasted by her cone-of-effect?"

"Alright, cut the chatter," Jace said sternly, but Tam could hear him smiling.

4

On the bridge, Captain Dav'i had a headache from the constant blips and lights that strobed across his console. "Give me an update Commander," he said, and rubbed his forehead.

"Our fighters have successfully engaged the corvettes," Plessis said, cracking her knuckles again. "I doubt they'll cause much of a problem. It's more the construction drones that are doing the real damage."

"Sensors, what are you seeing from the mining frigates?" Dav'i asked. He caught the eye of a petty officer at-the-ready and made a drinking gesture in front of his mouth. The petty officer quickly exited the bridge.

"The two mining frigates are holding position," Du Mon replied. "I've got an officer watching for any missile launches. It'd be the perfect time for it, while the laser batteries are targeting the drones."

"How's the armour holding, Commander?"

"We've lost pressure on one of the outer crew sections," Plessis said. "Thirteen spacers reportedly missing. The pressure locks sealed correctly though, so we've only lost access to that section of quarters."

Dav'i accepted the foil packet that the petty officer returned with. He unfastened the cap, and sucked on the slightly saline water inside.

"Are the construction drones going to be much more of a problem?" he asked.

"We've cleared 80% of the confirmed targets," Plessis said. We've lost the rearmost sensor array, however, so we're probably missing some data."

"We've just lost an *Invigilator*," Du Mon said.

"Instruct the other fighters to keep a wide berth," Captain Dav'i said. He looked at the console screen and sighed. "This is going to cost a fortune."

Plessis's console barked a warning, and she quickly began shouting instructions to the laserteams. "Heavy-ordinance missiles in-bound from deep-space," she declared loudly. "Targeting operators are to prioritise incoming missiles on the starboard. Launch anti-missiles when ready."

Dav'i brought up the list of laser turrets currently in operation. "Helm, accelerate the ship's rotation up to three gravities."

"Aye, captain," Dimi responded. A klaxon alarm sounded, and the new G-forces pushed Dav'i deep into his command chair. On his console, six large red triangles were accelerating towards *Socrates.*

"They calculated that well," he said, a tone of admiration creeping into his voice. "There are only four laser installations remaining in quadrant I of the ship, which they're aiming for." He checked the ship's rotation on his console.

"Dimi, assume that the missiles will hit us, and ensure that quadrant III is hit."

"Will do captain," said Dimi. He hunched his shoulders. The gravity lifted slightly, as Dimi corrected the rotation of the ship with the incoming missiles' speed.

"Lieutenant Mith, coordinate an evacuation of personnel from the outer decks of quadrant III, to the spine."

The young Lieutenant was chewing her bright red lower lip. She saluted and began shouting into her own console over the bridge sounds.

"The corvettes are targeting the engines, captain," Du Mon announced. "They're using their scoops to chip away at the tail spine. The construction drones have punched out the sensors at the rear of *Socrates*, so the automated lasers can't shoot them."

"Can the fighters handle it?"

"Eight of our fighters remaining, four corvettes remaining."

"Tell *Sullivan* to tuck in under our engines, have her broadcast her sensor data to us, and then reroute that to the laser batteries."

"The data won't be perfect, Captain. They'll be shooting mostly blind because of the delay."

"That's okay, we just want to scare them."

"All crew, brace for impact, ten seconds!" Plessis shouted from her console.

"Tell fighters to spread out," Dav'i yelled. "Get clear of *Socrates*."

"Warheads will hit quadrant III," Dimi announced.

"Counter-missiles away," Plessis said.

"Still evacuating!" Lieutenant Mith shouted.

Travelling at 15 km/s, the six Earth-Lunar missiles dropped military-grade counter-measures. Each missile jettisoned thirty superheated pellets out into space, each one a tempting target for the *Socrates's* counter-missiles.

In the deep silence of space, the *Socrates*' counter-missiles met with the guild's missiles. Two of the counter-missiles missed. Sensing that they had overshot their target, they detonated a second afterwards. Each of the missiles were successfully hit, and erupted into a cloud of liquid-metal debris that immediately cooled again. *Socrates'* automated debris lasers melted the incoming fragments down, disintegrating them as quickly as the computer could target them.

Unfortunately, a piece of metal debris, approximately ten centimetres in diameter, connected with the tail portion of *Socrates* and bore a hole through five metres of titanium plating. The rear of *Socrates* kicked like it had been punched by a giant, and several steel girders bent and buckled from the sudden movement.

"We've lost air pressure throughout quadrant III," Mith said. "We've lost an estimated fifty personnel who didn't evacuate in time. First-response teams are standing by."

Dav'i let out a breath. His teeth hurt from grinding them. *After six hundred Martian years of developing spacecraft,* he realised gloomily, *the best weapon is still ramming a target with mass.*

"Send in the first-response team," he said.

"Captain," said Plessis. "Fighters have destroyed the last of the corvettes with missiles. We'll be within missile range of the enemy's mining frigates in three minutes."

"Perfect," said Dav'i. "Have our fighters target any automated laser batteries first, and then we'll begin our bombardment."

"The enemy frigates are broadcasting their surrender," Plessis said. She turned to him, eyebrows raised, and they shared a silent, morbid joke.

"Are you certain about that Commander?"

"Apologies, Captain." Plessis typed rapidly on her console, and executed a delete command into the computer's communication log. "My mistake."

"That's quite alright commander," said Dav'i with a wide grin. "We can't help it if the surrender never reached us."

5

Prince Du Mon had seen people die in the military simulations that the consul had forced him to sit through. There'd also been more visceral, interactive simulations that the military had put him through. He'd also seen plenty of dramas about his father's war exploits.

When people died in the simulations, or in the dramas, they usually did it heroically. Even the villains or the enemy soldiers might do a little pirouette when shot. The blood might squirt, or splatter, or gore, but there was a meaning behind it: *they stood in our way, so we killed them.* Or, *someone dies, but it means the others live.*

There was none of that grandeur when Jason died.

"Jace has been hit!" Tam shouted loudly in his ears.

The Senior Ensign officer in front of Du Mon slammed his fist against the console. "I've lost Pilot 1," he said. "Vitals are gone. No heart rate, 2% brain activity."

In his ears, Du Mon could hear Tam swearing as he chased down a corvette. The camera feed from Jace's fighter had gone black. Du Mon rewound the footage as the captain coordinated a missile barrage against the enemy frigates. The last ten seconds of Jason's life flashed up on Du Mon's console. He watched, transfixed.

It was a quiet moment, as a corvette's invisible scoop swept across Jace's cockpit. He probably didn't realise what had happened, or why he had died. As the prince watched, the feed scrolling forwards in slow-motion, the tight polymers of Jace's flight suit unravelled from his arms and chest. The pressurised cooling liquid from his spacesuit exploded into the zero-gravity cockpit like snow. The non-metallic components in the cockpit turned into a fine-grained sand.

The mining scoop technology solved a lot of problems: break down ice and minerals, then collect the dust, and sift it back at a mining frigate. However, the technology was never intended to be used on a person.

The cockpit began to rust around Jace as the reinforced steel was broken down at a much slower pace and pulled towards the scoop. Du Mon willed himself to look away, but his gaze remained locked on the console in horror. In a few seconds, Jace's spacesuit had failed in a vacuum. The gasses in his blood expanded. His body ballooned outwards, ripping through the tattered remains of his suit. His skin cracked. Body fluids leaked from the dried skin and muscle, and then froze. The video feed cut off as the reinforced circuitry inside the vehicle was broken down.

Du Mon vomited into the air above his console, much to the disgust of the bridge officers. He excused himself, and pushed away awkwardly from the console, nearly running into the door.

"We're at battle stations, don't abandon your post!" Plessis yelled.

Du Mon punched the bridge's door control, and barely made it to vacuum-sink down the hallway before he vomited again.

With a shaking hand, he pulled a wet-wipe from the

dispenser above the toilet, and cleaned his lips with it. The sink hissed and sucked.

Jace's final moments, floating there, were burned into his memory. There was nothing dignified about it. He hadn't even resembled a human. He imagined the rapidly-freezing body, trapped in the wreckage of Jace's fighter, hurtling out into space forever.

Du Mon tried to compose himself. In the mirror, his skin looked unhealthy. He was sweating, and his hair was matted. He took a paper towel, and dabbed his face. Then he threw that in the sink as well.

In the hallway outside the combat-toilet stood Consul Barclay, waiting.

"Are you alright, my prince?" asked the towering figure.

"Fine, Barclay. Just a bit shaken," said Du Mon. *He looks disgusted at me. Like I've failed him.*

"Do you need me to get you anything?"

The Consul spoke quickly, following Du Mon as he made his way back to the bridge. When Du Mon opened the bridge door, a senior ensign was clearing the air of his vomit with a portable-vac.

"Sorry about that," he mumbled.

The captain shook his head. "Lieutenant Du Mon, you can focus your console on trying to crack the Earth-Lunar scramble code that they're using." There was an edge of annoyance, but the captain quickly turned around, focussed on the next task.

"Captain, if I may?" interrupted the consul from the bridge's doorway. The giant had stuck his foot across the threshold, preventing the door from cycling closed automatically. The door was beeping in annoyance.

The captain looked up at the consul, surprised.

"Civilians aren't permitted here," he said simply. "Exit the bridge immediately."

"But if I might make a suggestion about how to best help His Highness?" the consul offered.

The captain laughed. "No, you most certainly may not."

The Consul stood there for a moment, expressionless. He stared at Dav'i for several good seconds, and then pulled his foot from the door, allowing it to cycle shut. Several young ensigns looked at the prince with a mixture of delight and shock.

The prince felt his cheeks burning, and turned back to his console. He booted up the decryption software and focused intently on scrubbing the enemy's radio frequencies with it.

"Senior Ensign Yap take over fighter control," the captain said.

The man wielding the liquid-vac beamed with excitement, and quickly returned to his own console.

6

Tam Sunter had stopped breathing properly, but he knew his flight suit was working perfectly. He'd seen the corvette arc back around abruptly while Jace was trying to get a missile lock. Jace hadn't reacted quickly enough, and the corvette had managed to pull a turn that it shouldn't have. *Not with its specifications.*

Tam had shouted a warning and rolled to the port, out of the corvette's flight path. Jace had reacted a moment too late, and had banked to starboard.

Tam still wasn't sure if the corvette pilot had managed to calculate a trajectory to hit Jace with the scoop, or if it was just dumb luck, but they'd succeeded in catching Jace for several seconds before quickly veering away.

If Jace had been aboard the *Socrates*, the ablative armour of the ship would have taken the brunt of the attack, and he might have walked away from it. Unfortunately, the *Invigilator Mk-II*'s viewport didn't do much to stop atomising devices.

Tam had watched, helplessly, as Jace's fighter had stopped responding a few seconds after he'd pulled away from the scoop's beam. A feeling of fear and disgust wedged itself deep in his gut. Jace's ship continued to sail under the impulse of a single engine. Tam saw the fighter spin slowly as it spluttered and kicked, out and out towards Jupiter's orbit.

Socrates's airlock suddenly hissed open above him, and an engineer reached a hand down to assist him out of the fighter. Tam ripped off his helmet, and gasped for air.

"I'm fine, leave me be," he said. Tam fiddled with his crash netting, but his hands were shaking as he tried to unfasten it.

The engineer reached down and unclipped it for him. Tam kicked the fighter's controls in front of him, hard.

"I said I'm fine," he snapped, and scrambled out of the fighter. He threw his helmet at the engineer, winding him.

Along the launch bay, the other pilot's cockpits were ejected from their fighters as they docked, and rose up through the bay's floor. In his peripheral, he saw Jenna scrambling out of her cockpit to his left, and moving towards him. She called out his name, but he pretended not to hear her.

Instead, he picked up his pace, and exited the launch bay. He turned the corner and quickly made his way towards his quarters. They'd completed the mission, somehow. His training had kicked in, and he'd assumed command of the mission. Now the mission was over, however, and he wanted to break something.

He passed a group of three spacers in the corridor, who were heading towards the launch bay. They gossiped loudly. One of them, who was bald and missing several teeth, was complaining to a gaunt, skinny one. "Where are we gonna' sleep now the quarters are a pile of rubble?"

"I'm sure our ensign'll find us somewhere to bunk."

They saw him coming from the other direction and threw lazy salutes. He ignored them, instead of saluting back, and kept pace towards his quarters.

"Bloody rude," said the bald one, still loud enough that Tam could hear him.

"Maybe he's upset," said the gaunt one as Tam rounded the corner. "One of the fighters decided to have a close look at a scoop."

"So what? I lost my step-brother to those missiles, and you don't see me weeping."

"You hated him, that's why."

Tam arrived at his quarters with clenched fists. He kicked the door, and then punched in the code. It locked behind him. His bunk netting had come dislodged in the battle. He hung it back on its hooks in the ceiling. He opened his workstation desk, and saw that his pictures and other trinkets had all been thrown about.

Tam opened the cabinet under the console. The antique whiskey that he kept there had toppled sideways, but thankfully the glass hadn't broken. He stood up and removed the stopper from the bottle.

"Here's to you Jace," he said. The door buzzed, and he took a sip straight from the bottle. The door buzzed again.

"Go away," Tam yelled.

"It's Jenna," came a voice from behind the door.

"I said go away," he repeated, and took another swig. The door buzzer went off a third time, and he resisted the urge to throw the bottle.

"What do you want, Jenna?" he stopped the bottle again, and placed it out of sight in his workstation desk, and closed the lid.

"I just need to talk," she said.

Tam breathed deeply, and counted to ten. He willed

himself to calm down, and then opened the door. He'd barely opened it, before Jenna had leapt across the threshold and wrapped him up in a bear hug.

"I'm sorry," she said, and he could hear from her voice that she'd been crying.

"There's nothing to be sorry for," he said, refusing to look at her. His voice sounded flat, he realised. He tried to pull away and compose himself, but Jenna held on.

"I'm so sorry," Jenna repeated.

Tentatively, he returned the hug. Tam felt tears beading in his eyes. He shook his head, but the salty water clung to his face just as resolutely as Jenna, and trailed to the side of his face.

"I'm pissed Jenna," Tam said. "Why'd he die?"

"I don't know," Jenna said. She pulled away and wiped her face.

"Why didn't he turn in time?"

"Maybe he was distracted. Maybe the corvette pilot was the best damn pilot in the solar system and Jace met his match. Deimos knows what actually went on."

"The corvette didn't have a great pilot," Tam replied. There was a sharp pain in his throat that was making it difficult to speak. "I shot him down a minute later. Pathetic. Maybe if someone else had been coordinating the fighters. Comms was distracted. That prince probably didn't warn us in time."

"You don't know if that's true."

"He didn't help at all. It was like flying blind. Who put him in charge?"

"Can we recover Jace's fighter?" Jenna asked gently.

"I'll ask the captain," he said. "Or at the very least, we can track it and I'll get it after the debriefing."

"Will he let you do that?" Jenna asked, wiping away a tear. It floated through the air and hung suspended between the two of them.

"I think so," Tam replied. "I can be pretty convincing."

7

Commander Plessis had served with Captain Dav'i for the past five Martian years, and had turned down three promotions in that time. They'd served together for 3 years during the war, then for another 2 years while Earth and Mars negotiated a shaky cease-fire. In all that time, she had learned one irrefutable fact: Dav'i always ran his important meetings after a meal.

"Before we begin business," the captain said from the head of the table, "I order everyone to fill their plate. Doesn't matter if you feel hungry or not. Eat up."

The senior officers of the *Socrates* sat around the table, in order of rank. At the captain's encouragement, everyone dutifully began to fill their plates with the food arranged on the long, ceramic table.

The officer's chef had smuggled a giant red hen aboard, and then somehow chemically cooked the entire creature. It had sat proudly in the middle of the table, until the lieutenants worked up the courage to begin dismantling it onto their plates.

"I thought they were endangered?" Mith whispered across the table.

"I'm fairly sure they are," Plessis smiled.

Dav'i shrugged. "Sometimes you have to bend a rule to make sure morale is up. Hey, Pilot Sunter! That's not enough,

I ordered you to fill your plate."

Tam looked at the captain, deadpan, and then pulled another substantial piece of meat from the hen.

"And you better finish that plate young man," said Dav'i. IIe twirled his moustache while the rest of the crew piled up their plates. Satisfied, he stood, and held up his foil packet that had '*mulled wine*' printed on the front.

"A toast," the captain said, suddenly sombre. "To those who fell today."

The men and women gathered around the table rose quickly, holding aloft their own packaged beverages.

"I've seen many good astronauts die in the line of duty," he said, carefully looking each of them in the eye. "We didn't lose a great amount of people today—" his eyes locked with Tam's. "—But Phobos, we lost some quality folk."

Tam visibly flinched, and Plessis saw the tears welling up in his eyes. *I wonder if the captain really can read minds,* she thought. *Or perhaps he's just had to give this speech too many times.*

"To our colleagues," Dav'i said, and took a swig from his sachet. The room echoed the toast, and then sat down and began eating. Plessis picked at her petri-grown beef, and ate her hydroponic salad in silence, watching the others.

She tried to remember the faces that had sat around this table at her first officer's debrief, but could only recall a few of them. The faces around the table changed frequently: people were killed, and others were quickly promoted to replace them. She looked in Tam's direction. He picked at his food, despite the captain's warning, and looked like he might burst into tears at any moment.

She knew of some other officers who had transferred to

a better life. The previous commander had almost whistled and danced aboard his retirement shuttle.

Some had been idealistic enough to one day get promoted to their own vessel. *Mith seems eager,* Plessis thought. The beautiful lieutenant hung from the captain's words, as he told a story. She was subconsciously mimicking his body language. *Mith would be better-off finding a nice position as an administrator.*

Tam Sunter and Prince Du Mon sat a seat apart from each other. Both were silent as the table swapped stories from the skirmish. One young lieutenant asked Tam about the dogfight in space, but Tam just gave him a look that could have frozen the sun.

As the meal went on, and new foil packets of alcohol were opened, the talking at the table grew more and more boisterous. Tam Sunter was staring daggers at the prince, who chewed on obliviously. The captain stood at the hour mark, exactly. However, Plessis was probably the only person who noticed.

"A word of advice, to all my aspiring captains out there," Dav'i said with a broad grin. "Never, ever, do something serious on an empty stomach. That includes fighting, hatching plans, or love-making."

A hearty cheer went up from the senior officers.

"Now then, Lieutenant Mith. Give us a status report on the damage we've sustained."

Mith consulted the tablet in front of her for a moment, and then stood at-ease, with her hands folded behind the small of her back.

"Damages to our ablative armour were significant," she began. "The miners knew how to cut away at us, and they did a good job of trying to cripple the *Socrates*. While I don't doubt the intelligence of some of the mining guild's leaders, I would suggest that they might have had some—" she searched for the right words, "—*external consultation* about how to best hurt the *Socrates*."

"You suspect that Earth's military might have given them a few pointers?" Dav'i asked.

"Well, they knew where we would be, and our flight path. They didn't just launch the missiles, or the corvettes, or the mining drones. They did all three simultaneously, and each of them worked as a diversion while the next stage of the attack occurred."

"I see," Dav'i replied. "That point actually intersects with a concern that I have, but we'll return to it. Continue."

"It seems that a portion of the mining droids were programmed to specifically target our rear sensors and laser batteries—" Mith said.

While she spoke, every male in the room was invested in each syllable she uttered. *Maybe she will make a great captain,* Plessis thought, *so long as the women serving under her don't cut her throat from pure jealousy.*

"—then the drones targeted the structural spine that joins our engines and fission reactor to the rest of the ship. They were trying to cripple us."

"A solid tactic," Plessis added. "Earthen military used to invest heavily in trying to take out Martian fission reactors. They're a well-known weakness in the *Socrates*'s design line. They also see them as a form of heresy."

"Targeting our engines doesn't necessarily mean they had an Earthen tactician advising them though," the captain thought aloud. "They could just read up on some war history to know that. Sorry, please continue Mith."

"Repair crews will need to reweld the spine in the targeted areas. The drones drilled through about four metres of armour, conduits and piping. I've limited us to about 40% engine power, because I don't want to overload the infrastructure we have left. We also can't trust the computer to pressurise that part of the vessel correctly. We might waste oxygen by accidentally venting it into the spine of the ship."

"Send an order to the spacer repair-teams," the captain said to Plessis. "They'll need to prep for zero-gravity welding. Promise them extra alcohol rations, since they'll miss out on a shift of sleep."

Plessis looked at her tablet, and it woke up. She tapped on the table, and her eyes twitched across its surface. The tablet obeyed, and sent the message.

"At last roll call we lost our Squadron Leader, eight ensigns, and fifty-eight spacers from various decks. The main losses were concentrated in quadrant III when the ship depressurised. The rescue teams have recovered twenty-six bodies, but we're missing the rest who were pulled into space, plus the body of Squadron Leader Jason Warsch. The other bodies are retrievable, but not his. We're currently tracking the trajectory of his fighter, which is en route to Jupiter under its own momentum."

Tam Sunter stood up and saluted respectfully. The captain gestured to him.

"Yes, do you have something to say Squadron Leader Sunter?"

The man locked eyes with the captain, and opened his mouth, but the words weren't audible. A pang of sympathy gripped Plessis. She remembered that feeling. Tam coughed loudly. He held up a hand and breathed in a ragged breath, like he'd been punched in the gut.

"Wait until the end of the meeting," the captain said sympathetically. "I'll give you my answer once everyone has all the information."

8

The meeting continued, but Du Mon couldn't pull his eyes away from Tam Sunter, who sat bereaved.

Commander Plessis had taken over the discussion. "We have to ask ourselves why a private space company would attack a military vessel."

"Maybe they had a death-wish," Dimi piped up.

"Assuming they didn't," she continued, "my guess is that mining out here is far less lucrative than the Earth-Lunar alliance originally estimated it would be."

"I reckon they thought they'd disable us easily," Lieutenant Mith suggested. "Hence the minefield of explosives in our flightpath to try and cripple us early. If they'd disabled us and taken *Socrates*, we'd have been worth a hundred trillion yuan in metal, water, and oxygen to them. Not to mention the two mining frigates we have, which they could take to bolster their productivity."

"The lure of the prince is probably what tipped the balance for them," said Plessis. "The ransom of a crew, plus a royal, would be sizeable. They'd have to be clever about how they collected that ransom, but it's possible."

"It's still too risky," the captain said. He slurped his gelatinous soup. "It doesn't add up."

"Desperation doesn't need to make logical sense," Plessis suggested.

"For the time being, we'll need to be wary of any other ships that they might have in the Kuiper Belt," the captain said. He pushed his soup away with a clatter. "The next agenda item is that High Command has instructed us to divert course."

Tam looked up suddenly. Du Mon saw the fear in his eyes.

"To where, Captain?" Tam asked.

"We'll be dipping under the asteroid belt to intersect the Ceres planetoid mine and construction plant."

"Has there been some sort of threat to the Martian operations there?" Lieutenant Mith asked.

"Forty-six hours ago, they sent out a panic alarm for five minutes, and then suddenly ceased communications," said Plessis. "No contact since then, and some important people who own stocks at those mines are getting twitchy."

"Nothing worse than a twitchy politician," Captain Dav'i agreed.

"Could it be the Earth-Lunar Guild again?" asked Dimi. "They've already demonstrated that they're desperate enough to attack an armed vessel. Attacking an isolated, and relatively unarmed mining outpost could also be a tantalising option for them."

"We don't have much information," the captain replied. "So, once we finish patching ourselves together here, we'll push out to intersect with Ceres as soon as we can."

"Will the repairs be made in time?" Tam Sunter asked, a bit too quickly. "I mean...it could take a few standard shifts to repair the damage to *Socrates*, and—"

"—we can't be certain of what happened," the captain interrupted. "We could arrive there, and find that the sensors have malfunctioned. We might arrive and find the

Earth-Lunar guild has put people to work loading up their own ships instead of ours. Deimos knows it could be anything. We're the closest ship though, despite repair times, so we might as well not keep them waiting."

The captain stood and gestured for Tam Sunter to stand also. He did, with a confused look sketched on his face.

"Now, to answer your real question: how will we be able to collect Fighter 1 while carrying out repairs? The short answer is, we won't. In fact, our orders are to fly out to Ceres as soon as feasible."

Tam's shoulders slumped slightly.

"Don't look at me like that. I haven't finished," the captain said. "Protocol allows me to send out a scouting mission ahead of us while we conduct repairs. Lieutenant Mith realised that if we plot the current trajectory of Fighter 1, you should be able to catch it only a standard day's flight out from Ceres."

Tam Sunter threw a salute. His eyes welled-up, and his arm shook slightly. "Thank you, sir."

"You are hereby given command of the reconnaissance mission out at Ceres," the captain saluted in return. "Once you collect Fighter 1, plot a fly-by past Ceres and report back anything strange your sensors pick up. You'll report directly to Commander Plessis, and no one else. Have a seat Sunter. We'll assign you another officer to help with the retrieval." The captain turned back to the rest of the table.

The prince suddenly found himself standing. "Sir, I'd like to accompany him."

The captain reached over and took a scrap of meat still clinging to the red hen. "Oh?"

"Jason was a close friend of mine back at the academy. I

was in charge of fighter coordination when he died, so I feel responsible for his death—"

"Well, in that case, permission denied," the captain said simply.

A few people shifted uneasily in their chairs. The captain, unconcerned, kept chewing as he looked at his plate. Plessis was nodding her head.

"You'd better give the captain a different reason," she offered gently. "He won't let you go if you blame yourself for the death of a subordinate."

"First lesson of leadership," Captain Dav'i said without looking up. He wiped the oil and gristle away from his moustache.

"He was a good friend and colleague," the prince tried again.

"Now you're just copying Tam Sunter's answer," the captain said. "You're a target for those Earth-Lunar terrorists you know, I need a better reason than that. Especially if I have to explain to your father how you got yourself killed, ten thousand kilometres away from my care."

If I had been paying better attention, I would've noticed the Earth-Lunar guild ahead of us. If I were better at comms, maybe Jason would be alive still.

"I don't think we should trouble the prince," Tam suggested in the silence. "I have several pilots who I'd work well with on a reconnaissance mission."

The captain ignored him. "Well, Your Grace?"

"I haven't had a chance to do a special mission like this," Du Mon said. "It feels important to me, because I knew Jason. It's more than that though. I'd like to actually complete a mission, and do it well, unlike this afternoon."

The captain finally looked up at the prince, and his eyes were gleaming. "A chance to prove yourself then? Commander, can you swing that in your report?"

"I think I can," Plessis said. She cracked an actual smile.

Tam's arms were crossed. He shrugged without uncrossing them. "Looks like we'll be a team. It's a shame the circumstances aren't happier."

"A shame," Du Mon repeated.

"Unfortunately, there is one final agenda item," the captain said, gesturing for them to sit again. He shook his head, pulled back his chair, and turned to examine the digital display of the solar system behind his chair. "I've got good reason to believe that there's a mole aboard."

The younger lieutenants murmured to each other quietly. A few of the more senior staff, however, just nodded.

"What makes you suspect that captain?" Dimi asked at the opposite end of the table.

"The fact that the enemy knew our flight path, and had enough time to lay a makeshift minefield directly in front of us," Dav'i replied. He turned around to look at them, and his face was a vivid shade of red.

"They knew *exactly* where we would be, dammit. They knew Du Mon was stationed on this vessel, which is a military secret. Now, it's possible that someone in High Command is a turncoat, but it's far *more* likely that we have someone onboard who broadcasted our coordinates and trajectory towards that little welcome party we ran into."

The captain was puffing from fury, so he nodded to Plessis and sat heavily in his chair.

"While the spacers are busy repairing the structural damage," Plessis began, "we'll do a top-down search of the crew's personal transmissions, to check if the transmission came from us. I will be checking your radio logs, and the captain's, for any evidence of tampering. Those of you with comms knowhow will check the logs of the comms team, and the comms team will go through the logs of everyone else, including myself."

"For the time-being, we're going to block any personal transmissions," the captain added. "Hopefully, no one's missing their mummy."

The captain dismissed the senior staff, and Du Mon suddenly realised how weary he felt. Standing from the table, he exited the room ahead of the others, and headed for his quarters.

Thankfully, he wasn't cornered by the consul on his way to the room. Arriving at his door, he glanced at the consul's room behind him. The door remained shut.

Keying his personal code into the door, he stepped inside and found Harmony exactly where he'd left her: reading on his bunk. She had a habit of tapping her foot in rhythm with her reading. *Tap, tap, tap.* As he approached, however, Du Mon noticed that her face was red from crying.

"Welcome home honey," she said, and sniffed.

"Thanks for staying up. Sad story?"

"Yeah," she replied. "It's about this young couple who can't be together because their parents are at war."

He sat on the bed and pulled his boots off with some effort. As he removed the second one, he felt her short arms encircle him from behind. She rested her chin on the top of his head.

"You look like you had a difficult couple of shifts," she said sincerely. All traces of her usual sarcastic wit had vanished.

"Yeah, I saw something pretty gruesome." Du Mon looked at his hands while he spoke, it felt easier than meeting her eyes.

"Are you going to be okay?" she asked.

"I'll be fine, I think."

"Death is never pleasant," she said. A reassuring hand was placed on his shoulder. "I've had this conversation with many people. Even veterans struggle to cope with some of the things they're forced to see."

There was a pang of jealousy, as Du Mon remembered that Harmony would have sat in other officer's rooms, just like this one. He'd managed to forget that small fact for some time now.

"How can I lead these people one day?" The disgust he'd repressed since the debriefing reared its head again. "I can't even handle watching one person die."

"That just means you have empathy," Harmony said. She smiled warmly, and shook a ring of curls over her shoulder. "Empathy is never a bad thing to have."

"Have you thought about what I offered?" he asked suddenly.

Harmony took a deep breath, and shrugged.

"You're not the first person to offer me a new life Du. Every other officer with a decent heart wants to 'rescue' me. I think you probably just feel guilty having me."

The prince shook his head. "Not in the slightest. I'm actually just very self-centred, petty, and I don't like it when you mention other guys. It's pretty poor bedside manner."

Harmony laughed at that. "Well at least you're honest about it."

"So, what's your answer?"

"My answer is wait-and-see, Your Grace. We'll return to Mars after this mission, you'll get stationed aboard another ship, and then that will be that. You'll meet other lovely ladies, I'm sure. The Companion Guild values your patronage too much to leave you stuck with a girl who's lost her teeth to scurvy or something."

Du Mon looked firmly into Harmony's green eyes, and she looked back into his, unflinching. "I'm not talking about getting some quick fix here Harmony. I'm talking about companionship."

"You can always buy companionship," Harmony replied lightly, but when she saw that he wouldn't back down, she grew serious. "Fine. You can believe your little fantasy of sweeping me away to a life of luxury. I've heard it a dozen different ways Du." She sighed, and picked up her tablet. "At the end of your service, you'll be married off to a lovely lady in a dress. She'll probably be related to an important diplomat from the Earth or the Moon. You'll kick and cry foul, and then your father will beat you. Then you'll give me a half-smile apology and I'll be on the next ship out to the belt."

A single tear pooled in her left eye, but Harmony ignored it.

"It's best not to make promises like that anymore Du. In fact, I forbid it from now on. I've seen the pattern, and while you're a nice guy, I doubt you have the guts to throw away your prepared slice of the empire for little old me. I'd consider your proposal better if you promised to run away with *me* instead."

Du Mon got up from the bunk, his ears burning. "You want me to run away with you?" He sputtered, growing angrier. "To where? Some small mining colony? That's barely better than dying."

"I think we should just think about other options."

"What other options Harmony? Listen to yourself, where could I go and still have a decent life? In fact, you could probably get deported to the *Montessori* if people found out you were suggesting I abandoned my place in the family."

Harmony stood up on the bunk, so she was eye-level with him.

"Go ahead then, deport me. I've done my rounds on a mining frigate, I'm prepared for what goes on down there. At least then you'll have shown your true colours, Your Grace. We'll both know that I'm no princess when I end up lying in the arms of a toothless spacer."

The prince ground his teeth in fury, but the image of Harmony with another man was sufficiently disgusting to bring him to his senses.

"You're going to eat those words when we get back to Mars," he said. "I'll stand up to my father and carve out something for myself. I've got bigger plans than you think."

"I doubt it Du," Harmony said. She stepped off the bed gracefully, and flounced out of his quarters. "Feel free to prove me wrong though."

9

Consul Barclay knocked lightly on the prince's door. He sighed. It was an archaic habit from his youth that he couldn't shake. He pressed the intercom instead. Barclay waited politely for a moment, and then pressed it again. *Perhaps His Grace is distracted again.*

Barclay keyed his personal code into the panel beside the door, and it slid open for him. The lighting in the quarters had been turned to half-brightness. The prince was buried face-down in his pillow, arms by his side.

"It's time for your lessons, Your Grace." Barclay manually pulled the door shut behind him, out of habit again, and winced as the door's stepper motor groaned in protest.

The prince looked up from his pillow and glared at the old man from the corner of his eyes.

"Don't break my door, you luddite."

"My apologies Your Grace. Whatever happened to a good, old-fashioned manual door?" He pulled out a stool that was stored flush against the wall, unfolded it, and sat down at the foot of the prince's bunk. "You missed breakfast, so I asked the officers' chef to package some of his signature petri-grown beef. The spices on this are really quite excellent, it reminds me of when we had vacuum-dried beef shipped in from Earth." He mimed wiping a tear from his eye with a long, bony finger. "Those flavours haunt me."

The prince, face-down, gestured to his work bench, and Barclay dutifully left the food there for him to pick at later. "Shall we begin our lesson for today, Your Grace?"

The prince sighed, and rolled over to face him. His face was flushed, and his almond eyes were red.

"My apologies," the consul said. "I can see I've somehow interrupted you. I can come back again when you're composed."

"No, it's fine Barclay." The prince sat up and wiped his nose with the back of his hand. "I mean, it isn't actually fine. I hate having to do lessons while I'm on duty. No one else loses a recreation shift because they have to study up."

"Please, use this." Barclay took off his satchel, and pulled out a bamboo tissue. The prince took it, and blew his nose.

"I'm afraid all great people dedicate their spare time to improve themselves. Being a life-long learner is about embracing the quiet moments you have, or carving out precious hours in your timetable to learn and grow as a person."

The prince didn't look at the consul, but instead spun around and lay down with his feet on his pillow. "Okay, Barclay. I have a lot on my mind though, so please cut your lesson down to an hour."

"Done, Your Grace." The consul pulled his touch tablet from his satchel, and lay it atop his lap. At fifteen, the prince had told him in no uncertain terms, *that model of a tablet is a relic now, just like you*.

Du Mon readjusted himself on his back, eyes closed, fingers-interlaced on his stomach, and his breathing slowed. The Artemis technique required a student to be perfectly at ease before the learning could begin. The Consul waited patiently, until the spaces between the prince's breaths were regular.

"How do you feel?" Barclay asked, consciously lengthening his syllables to a monotony.

"Comfortable," the prince replied.

"Do you remember what we discussed last lesson?" Barclay asked. He searched in his throat for the right timbre, the correct pitch.

"The beginning of the Earth-Lunar conflict," the prince's voice had also slowed. "When my great-grandfather chose to end the unfair trade agreements."

"What year was that, my prince?" the consul asked. He lowered the register of his voice slightly, and the prince frowned slightly. He mentally adjusted his tone. Finding the right tone of voice was akin to an artform.

"3015 CE, nearly 1000 Earth-years after the first colonists landed on Mars."

"Very good," the consul said. He felt it then. His voice became like liquid, and he let it drip through his throat, and into the correct register for Du Mon. After years of instructing the prince, his body instinctively knew that he'd arrived at the correct spot for the prince's mind and current mood.

"Can you hear me Du Mon?" he asked.

The prince nodded lethargically.

"Excellent," said Barclay. "Tell me, what is troubling you today?"

"I had a fight with Harmony," the prince mumbled.

"I'm sorry to hear that," Barclay said in a drawl. "What did you fight about?"

"She thinks I don't love her, but I do." The prince said. His voice sounded defensive, like a teenager caught writing a love letter. *Perhaps I misjudged his feelings for her.*

The consul frowned, and selected the soothing soundscape that he had written for the prince's thirteenth birthday. "Emotions are difficult to know for certain," he said to the young prince. "Perhaps she doesn't feel the same way?"

"I think she does," said the prince. His eyes moved rapidly under their lids, searching for the consul's voice, but unable to find him.

Not again, Barclay thought. He changed tactic. "Have you ever felt embarrassed about something?"

"Yes, plenty of times."

"When you look back at some of those times, do they now seem silly, trivial, or funny in hindsight?"

"Some of them yes, but recently not so much." The prince said wistfully.

"This feeling of affection that you had for Harmony: it was something that you felt in the past. Yesterday, last week. You don't feel that way anymore. How do you feel about Harmony?"

"I used to care for her deeply. I think I loved her, but I don't feel that way anymore," the prince repeated.

"Maybe you never really loved her. Do you think it was just hormones?"

The prince knitted his eyebrows together. "It felt real yesterday, I don't think I was imagining it."

"But you don't feel that way anymore, do you?"

"I don't feel that way anymore."

"I'm glad to hear that," the consul said. "Is there anything else troubling you?"

"There is," the prince said. His voice was becoming more childlike.

Even when he was young, Barclay wasn't interested in space, or space exploration. *The human mind is the final frontier*, he had realised long ago. *Discovering a new galaxy is miniscule next to the discovery of a new brain response. The mapping of galaxies is crude and lacklustre compared to the joy of mapping forests of neurons. To control the mind is to control everything.*

"I can't stop thinking about Jason dying, it's haunting me a lot."

The consul rubbed his temple and contemplated how to approach the problem.

"Are you still there?" the prince asked, his eyes searching more fervently through the skin.

"Of course I am," the consul said. He reached over and dimmed the lights more. "What happened to this Jason?" he asked.

"I think I killed him," the prince said.

"Why do you think that?"

"I heard some talk on the radio frequencies. Mining equipment, that sort of thing. I didn't think it was important, so I ignored it. Now I realise it was the bombs being told to arm themselves and hit the ship."

"Did a bomb kill this Jason person?" Barclay asked.

"No, his fighter was cooked."

The Consul pulled up the list of fighter pilots from the ship's manifest.

"How did he die?"

"I saw him balloon outwards. I think he might have popped. He melted into a puddle."

The Consul's eyes widened. *The prince's personality might be affected further if he keeps believing this.* He forced his voice to stay even.

"Are you certain he popped? People can't do that in the vacuum of space."

"Um...I think he did."

"You think you did? You were certain a moment ago."

"I can't remember it very well."

"In that case, when you wake up, you will remember Jace's death differently. What will you do?"

"I'll remember it different," the prince parroted.

"He died peacefully. What did he do?"

"He died peacefully."

"He died peacefully like he went to sleep. There was a single drop of blood, but it fled his nostril like an air bubble and poetically floated to the top of the cabin. Tell me how Jace died."

The prince recited the new mental image, and the consul listened carefully. He also censored any details that seemed too graphic. Once he was satisfied that the prince wouldn't picture Jace's death graphically anymore, he moved on to the cause of death.

"You can't remember the radio traffic," he told the prince. "You don't feel guilty about Jace's death."

He looked at the clock, ten minutes remaining. The Consul looked through his notes, which were being annotated by voice-recognition software on his tablet, densely summarising the topics they'd covered and the explicit questioning that the consul had asked.

Barclay went back through the questions, assessing the prince's answers, and making sure that their conversation had been correctly embedded just beneath the consciousness. He then wiped the record of the conversation from the prince's memory, and replaced it with a memory of learning about the Earth-Lunar Ceasefire Negotiation in 50ME, three years ago. He also implanted the idea that the prince had joked about being bored by modern history, to give the memory more flavour.

The wonderful thing about memory, thought the consul, *is how imprecise it is. You only need to fabricate a sentence of conversation, a smell here, a general image of where everything was, and you have a long-term memory ready to be believed.*

Satisfied with his work, Barclay closed his tablet and waited for the prince to drift back to consciousness. He smiled down at the sleeping prince and kissed his forehead, just as he had always done, since the prince was three years old.

10

Tam had accelerated away from the *Socrates* the same hour he'd received clearance. Du Mon sat beside him in the co-pilot's seat.

"How long have you been serving?" Du Mon asked.

Tam gave a loud and theatrical sigh, before swivelling in his crash netting to face the prince. "Look, it's great that you cared enough about Jace to come along. It really is. That doesn't mean we're going to be pals. We get Jace, we do the recon, we go home."

Du Mon glanced at Tam through the corner of his eye.

"Fine by me."

They flew in shifts for three days, accelerating as fast as practical beneath the Kuiper Belt, following the trajectory that *Socrates*'s computer had calculated for them.

Tam hummed a little ditty he couldn't remember the words to, about a young man who met a serpent on the Earthen sea.

"Can I tell you something?" the prince asked. He didn't wait for a reply. "Back on *Socrates*, when we left, I didn't say goodbye to the companion woman I've been going steady with.

"Harmony Xu, right?"

"That's her. I saw her lying there in my bed, but I just got dressed and I just left her there."

"Why would you do something like that?" Tam asked.

"I just didn't feel anything for her in that moment."

"That's cold, even for royalty." Tam said. "You'll be lucky if she wants to talk to you ever again."

"I guess."

Tam pointed. They could see Jace's fighter on sensors as it continued a slow, spiralling descent away from the solar system.

They'd been decelerating for the past hour once they'd calculated the fighter's distance and speed. The *Proctor*-class corvette that they flew was designed for medium-range missions, but not for comfort. Tam was tired, and despite the zero-gravity, his back hurt from being strapped into his flight chair for too long.

"Alright," he said. "Let's get this over with."

Tam brought them closer to Jace's fighter, as it continued its lazy spiral. Du Mon watched the instruments closely, occasionally kicking on the auxiliary thrusters to bring them a metre closer to the other vessel. He flicked on the safety switch above his console, and opened the shuttle doors with the bush of a button. An alarm beeped, but Tam ignored it.

The *Proctor* corvettes were versatile, and the middle portion of this one had been fitted with a cargo bay large enough to store an *Invigilator* fighter.

Du Mon screwed his helmet on, and switched off his console.

"Wish me luck," he said, and stepped into the airlock.

Tam nodded grimly, and turned back to his work. He heard the musical chime as the airlock finished depressurising.

"Can you hear me?" Tam asked.

"Roger," Du Mon replied.

"Stay in the airlock until I've brought the ship in. It's your own fault if I clip you with it."

Under his console, Tam tapped his left foot delicately on the pedal to fire the auxiliary thrusters on the corvette's starboard. The ship moved another metre, and he consulted the camera feed on his monitor. The fighter was still in one piece, more or less. He hit the thrusters again, and the fighter slipped halfway into the cargo bay.

"How's it look from your angle Lieutenant?"

"The fighter's right wing is too close to the cargo ceiling. You need to roll to port another ten degrees," Du Mon said.

Tam did it, and the ship appeared to rotate inside the cargo bay on his projected feed.

"How's that?" he asked.

"Another ten degrees," Du Mon said. "Sorry, my math was off."

He tapped the strange flight stick a touch to the left, and consulted the camera feed. The right wing was now pointed level with the floor. He tapped the auxiliary thrusters once more.

"Looks great," Du Mon said. "Close the cargo door and I'll strap it down.

Tam hit the safety switch on his console this time, and then closed the doors to the cargo bay. In the camera feed, he saw them inch shut slowly. The stars appeared to blink out as the door closed.

"Got him," Du Mon said. "I'll strap down the fighter."

Tam held the ship steady, matching the fighter's flightpath even though it was now trapped inside their corvette. Du Mon stepped out of the airlock, and opened a wall cabinet. He pulled out the tow straps, and began to tie-down the fighter to the floor of the cargo bay, using the hooks and rods built into the small depressions in its floor. Tam simply looked out into the infinite void between the stars, and waited.

The prince had cried for an hour after he climbed onto the fighter's nose and saw Jace's body. Tam piloted the corvette without much enthusiasm. *Why did you look inside, stupid?* Tam felt his own emotions rising up into his throat, and pushed them back down again. *I can't bear to see Jace like that. I'll look when the mission's over, and we're safe.*

Ceres was almost invisible as they approached it. A thin crescent of sunlight illuminated the edge of the nearly-round dwarf planet. Sections of Ceres had been carefully hollowed-out so that its orbit wasn't altered too significantly. From his vantage-point in the cockpit, Ceres looked nearly identical to Earth's moon. *Just not as busy*, Tam thought to himself.

At this time of year Ceres should have been a flurry of activity: the *Sullivan* and *Montessori* were scheduled to be processed here in a standard month, after all.

However, Ceres was dead. *As dead as Jace*, he thought grimly. The static of the radio droned monotonously. Du Mon had been scrubbing through the radio frequencies for the past three hours. No traffic on the usual Martian channels. Nothing on the inter-planetary frequencies. No flight control. Their computer couldn't detect any ships in orbit.

"I'm going to take us in closer," Tam said.

"Thank goodness," Du Mon replied.

Tam brought the corvette closer to the dark planetoid, firing the engines in reverse to slow their momentum. On its surface, large refining stations had been built. The skeleton of a half-constructed frigate still lay nestled in a land-dock on the surface. The ship's computer located a docking tower, and calculated rough landing data from it.

"The other docking towers have been destroyed," Tam said, studying the computer's readouts. "There should be three of them, but I'm only reading this one."

Du Mon tapped Tam's shoulder, and pointed to the viewport. Tam looked up. As Ceres spun on its axis, the sun, significantly smaller than it was on Mars, crept over the horizon. The light spilled over the ragged and industrialised surface of Ceres, illuminating the factories, exhaust vents, transport trucks, and its pitted surface.

"It's beautiful. In a sad, impoverished, abandoned kind of way," the prince said.

"It looked better in the past," Tam replied. "My grandfather worked out here."

"Have you visited Ceres before?"

"Just once, for a funeral."

As the sun's light grew brighter, however, Tam saw something else. A deep hole had been gorged into the surface of Ceres, at least eight kilometres across. As the light illuminated the rim of the hole Tam saw that it was deep, at least ten kilometres down.

"Was that hole there, the last time you visited?" Du Mon asked.

"It wasn't," Tam replied. "That's where the other docking towers used to be."

As they passed over the hole, a dull glow illuminated the walls of the disaster zone.

"Looks like the artificial core is in meltdown," Tam said. "The reactor might have been damaged."

The ship beeped a musical tune of success, announcing that the umbilical tube between the docking station and the corvette had successfully connected. Tam looked over the instruments again.

"The water lines aren't working properly," he said. "The system is refilling our fuel correctly, but the air and water aren't coming through."

"Let's go check it out."

"Hold it. I'm sending our logs to *Socrates*," Tam said. "In case we don't...you know."

"Oh," Du Mon said. He stood up and put his helmet on. There was an armoured cabinet at the rear of the cockpit. Du Mon pulled their guns from it. He threw Tam his rifle, but it flew through the air quicker than Du Mon anticipated, now that they weren't in absolute zero-gravity. It nearly hit Tam squarely on the face-plate.

"Watch it," the pilot said with a look of disdain.

They both stepped into the central airlock, and Tam told it to depressurise. He cycled the external door, and then pushed it open. The umbilical cord stretched out like the bellows of an accordion, out to the docking tower.

"Will the docking clamps hold, if everything else is broken?" Du Mon asked uncertainty.

"Of course they will," Tam replied, as confidently as he could.

He stepped into the umbilical tube, which gave way slightly under his weight. Du Mon climbed in behind him, and then closed the airlock door. The automatic lights weren't operating correctly. A single strip of LED glowed in the dark tunnel. Tam walked towards it, listening to his breath as it hissed in the claustrophobic dome of his helmet.

11

"What do you suppose happened?" Du Mon asked, as they climbed down the docking tower's emergency ladder.

"Judging by the impact crater back there, some sort of asteroid collision."

Du Mon pulled a face that he knew Tam couldn't see. "Seems a bit unlikely doesn't it?" he said. "I know Ceres was originally pitted from impacts, but something that large?"

They were both puffing from exertion. Du Mon looked down to see how far Tam was below him. It was a several-kilometre climb down to the surface of Ceres.

Days on Ceres were short, and the sun was already well beyond the horizon. Du Mon squinted at the blindingly-bright surface, towards the black pit that sank far below.

"Perhaps it was intentional?" Tam said. "You could redirect a medium-sized asteroid, and turn it into a fairly destructive weapon."

He had reached the surface, and unfastened his safety tether from the tower. He unslung his rifle, and was checking it by the time Du Mon joined him.

"I need a break before we scale that tower again," Du Mon said, rubbing his arms. He unslung his own rifle, pulled the bolt backwards, and examined the oxygen canister near the fuse.

"Let's hope we don't need to make a quick exit then," Tam

replied.

The broken, twisted intestines of the mining facility lay before them. Large industrial pipes ran the surface of Ceres in parallel lines like circuitry. Most were now cracked, their fluids spilled and frozen like snow. The ground shifted slightly under their feet, and in the distance a small housing bunker swayed and collapsed.

"That's new," Tam said.

"What's new?"

"There shouldn't be any quakes here."

They walked past a small booth that would have once been a cargo checking point. The main factory building was leaning precariously to the left, now barely held aloft by the twisted debris of conveyor belts and cargo trucks.

"The command centre was in this building, two levels down." Tam said. "We can probably piece together what happened, if we find their communications logs."

"We might even find survivors," Du Mon said hopefully.

Tam looked again at the dark blur on the horizon eight kilometres wide. "Yeah."

They arrived at a service airlock, peeled open like a can of tinned food. Du Mon reached out, and ran his gloved fingers along the control panel. His fingers came back coated in dust and frost that glittered.

"After you, Your Grace?" Tam offered with a small bow at the waist. His open palm was outstretched towards the wound in the service airlock.

"Dream on," Du Mon said.

"Suit yourself," Tam crouched low, and scurried through the door. Du Mon followed quickly behind. They hunkered down behind a cargo truck that had been crushed beneath an enormous iron support beam. Dust motes hung in the air, spiralling slowly and infinitely from their footsteps.

The chemical lights in the ceiling had failed. The sunlight from outside cast ice-cold shadows across the facility through shattered perspex windows.

"Those quakes really did a number on this place," Du Mon said, marvelling at the wreckage inside the sorting facility.

"Just have to figure out if a natural disaster caused it, or a rival mining conglomerate," Tam replied. "Huh, funny how difficult it is to tell those two things apart."

Tam moved forward as quickly as his suit would allow, and Du Mon followed. They bounded across the enormous sorting facility, each skip hurtling them forward metres at a time.

A long, enormous access tunnel rose upward from the sorting facility, large enough to permit two of the gigantic cargo trucks to drive side-by-side. Thankfully, Tam led them away from the man-made chasm, and down a small staff ramp beside it. As they descended deeper into the facility, Du Mon could feel the cold creep through the layers of pressure insulation in his spacesuit. They switched on their headlamps, and two circles of blue light painted the long-dead passageway.

"The heating has failed too." He said simply.

"Sort of," Tam replied. They took the ramp two storeys down, and exited through a wide concrete doorway painted a comforting blue. This level was a series of hallways and offices. Everything was silent and still.

"A lot of the heat was generated as a by-product from the foundries and smelting facilities. The factory is gone, and so is Ceres' ability to be liveable." Tam checked a corner quickly, rifle held upright and ducked back. "Wrong way," he said with a grin through his helmet.

"Just ask for directions, darling."

The other direction revealed a wide hallway, built for foot traffic.

"That's more like it," said Tam.

As they walked deeper into the facility, Du Mon felt more and more uneasy. A filing cabinet had been dropped in the process of being moved, and he took cover behind it.

"I don't like this, Sunter."

"The architecture is pretty hostile, I agree," Tam replied. "Look how low these ceilings are! It's like Earthen dwarves built it." Ahead, there was a door ajar, labelled *Exports Senior Officer*. He pushed the door open with his foot, and checked inside.

"We're too exposed," Du Mon hissed.

"There's no other option, unfortunately," Tam said, pulling his head back. "The command office was supposed to be easily-accessible. Besides, we're nearly there."

They passed a room labelled *Armoury*, and Tam checked it.

"Door's open." He disappeared inside, and Du Mon guarded the doorway from outside, tucked against the wall. Tam appeared again, and shook his head. "Riot gear left inside," he said. "But the weapons and guns are gone."

"They were expecting trouble," Du Mon said.

"Or they were sloppy keeping their armoury stocked."

The command office loomed at the end of the hallway, behind frosted perspex and waist-high polished concrete. Their headlights shone brilliantly against the polished concrete, and seemed to warp and vanish against the perspex.

"I always thought that was a really interesting way of interacting with light," Tam said, admiring the perspex.

"Tam, when's your birthday?"

"Next month, why?"

"I'll buy you an architecture program for your tablet, a really nice one with coloured pictures, so please focus."

"Yeah no worries," Tam said. He turned and flashed the prince a smile, but Du Mon caught the hesitation in it. *We're not in a spacecraft,* the prince realised. *He's afraid.*

Tam reached for the door handle, and then realised it wasn't there. Du Mon tilted his head down at the doorway. The metal of the door had been ripped away from the locking mechanism, and had crumpled like tissue paper. Tam checked his rifle again, unnecessarily, and then kicked at the door. It flew open. In the darkness there were the shapes of people. One man sat on a desk, slumped over. Another body was on the ground.

"Are they dead?" Du Mon asked.

Tam checked under the desks that were arranged along the perspex glass, and then answered.

"They're dead. Don't look at them."

Du Mon had already looked. The man sitting on the desk wasn't sitting. He had been wearing a space-suit when he died. His torso was propped up atop his desk. He stared down at the floor through his helmet, with eyes frozen in shock, probably searching for his legs.

The man on the floor had fared better. He'd died without any apparent wounds to his body. Du Mon searched the room with his headlamp, and found the body of a lady, curled up under her desk. Her eyes were closed, thankfully. Her chin waited gently on her knees. *That's how Harmony sits on my bunk.*

"They weren't shot," Tam said.

"They weren't hit by a landquake either Tam."

"The lady under there, she might have starved or frozen to death. Maybe she asphyxiated when the airlock was blown out. There's blood in her ears. Don't look too closely. This man here," he wedged a toe under the torso of the man on the floor, and pried him upwards slightly. "No idea."

"It's the man on the table that worries me," Du Mon said. "He died from something else entirely. What could do that to you?"

"There's a few weapons, or maybe an industrial accident could have caused it. Who am I kidding...he was ripped apart."

"Ripped in half," Du Mon repeated with a frown. "That strikes me as...very difficult to do."

The power wasn't working for any of the computers. Du Mon closed the door behind him, and Tam set to work tearing the office apart, searching for a map.

"We'll find comms and security records in the data centre," Tam said. "Or perhaps in the security offices themselves."

Du Mon saw an unlabelled door at the rear of the main office. He glanced back at Tam, whose head had disappeared inside a desk drawer.

"I'm going to look over here."

He pulled on the door's manual release, and it inched open with great effort. It was dark inside. His headlamp flashed across row after row of memory bank, tall and cold like statues. They glistened with ice. He tried the light switch near the doorway, but the chemical lights above him were dead. The power had failed here as well, sometime ago. The room was the size of a warehouse. It stretched far back, out of sight.

"I found the data centre, through the door at the back," Du Mon called. "There's so many memory banks. What did they need them for?"

"It'd be nearly impossible to stream anything from Mars out here," Tam replied. He grunted, and Du Mon heard something crash. "Too distant from Mars, and too slow to try and send it via radio. So, Ceres imported physical memory that contained portions of the internet, plus any recreational programs or dramas that they could manage."

Du Mon turned back towards the office, but in his periphery, he saw something move. He squinted.

"I found a facility map!" Tam called through the radio, startling him.

Du Mon clutched his heart, and looked back in the direction of the movement. There was a shape, something tall, that stuck out between the rows of memory banks. It moved again.

Reflexively, Du Mon ducked behind one of the machines. A beam of laser, white hot and perfectly straight, cut the air in an instant.

"Contact!" Du Mon heard himself scream into the suit's mic.

The laser swept to his hiding spot. Despite the vacuum, the memory unit behind his began to melt into slag. Du Mon ducked and weaved his way through the memory banks, putting distance between himself and the assailant.

"Hostile was at eleven o'clock when you stand at the doorway, currently firing a beam weapon at me." Sweat trickled along his forehead and into his eyebrows. His heartbeat hammered in his ears as he paused behind a memory bank, identical to the one he'd just hidden behind. The beam cut off abruptly. Du Mon quickly switched off his helmet lamp. He realised Tam was speaking.

"Hostile has moved," he was saying. "Did you identify him?"

"No," he panted. "It's using some type of laser weapon I don't recognise. Make your way south, towards me," Du Mon said. "They probably saw my headlamp and—"

Du Mon sensed something, and turned his head. Something tapped against the glass of his helmet. A yellow light beamed directly into his face. He screamed.

12

Captain Dav'i had called a special assembly of officers, as well as the consul. They gathered in the ship's briefing room. The space was decorated in white and black, shaped like a quarter-circle, and contained tiered seating for the officers along the curved portion of the room.

"The *Socrates* has received a report from Pilot Sunter and Prince Du Mon's corvette, who were sent on a reconnaissance mission," Captain Dav'i said, addressing the officers. "Their report tells us that Ceres has either been abandoned, attacked, or is currently not operating for an unknown reason. We will continue to Ceres in order to investigate the site more thoroughly."

Consul Barclay cleared his throat from the audience.

"Is there something you'd like to say, Consul?"

He stood and bowed. "Thank you, captain. Due to my station I'd like the record to show that I'm against the prince having been sent on a reconnaissance mission, especially without first consulting me. We've already been attacked with some measure of success, and I don't think it's wise to put His Grace in further danger without some measure of support. Especially now that these terrible matters have come to light."

Dav'i nodded. "I'll make sure the report mentions that. For the time being, we will be operating under our standing orders. Any further comments or questions before we begin?"

He looked around, but everyone else was silent. A few people shook their heads with disinterest. "In that case, let's begin the proceedings. As the senior staff were made aware, we've suspected for a time that there was a mole aboard the *Socrates*. Commander Plessis now believes that she has found the guilty party responsible."

Harmony felt every eye turn towards her as she stood before them. She forced herself to keep her head high, eyes level. Two burly spacers flanked her on either side.

"The trial will follow Martian democratic law," Captain Dav'i began. "Commander Plessis will act as the inquisitor for the purposes of this trial, and will bring her working case to this court for the purposes of cross-examining those she suspects to be guilty. If I determine a party to be guilty, then they will be locked in the brig until we return to Mars."

The commander stepped forward. The two spacers left Harmony, and guarded the exit. Plessis walked calmly with her hands clasped behind her back, circling.

"Ms Xu, eight days ago an encrypted radio message was dispatched from the private console in the prince's quarters. The message contained our then-coordinates, our trajectory, and our destination. It was written as a poem, so that the comm officer who inspected it didn't realise it contained confidential information. Did you send that message?"

"No, I did not," Harmony replied.

"At the time the message was sent, the prince was stationed on the bridge. He arrived at 0804, four minutes late for his shift. Can you tell us what you were doing at 0900 ship time, on that day?"

"I would have been in the prince's quarters, reading. Eight days ago is a long time. I may have gone for a walk to stretch my legs."

Dav'i frowned. "Before we continue this line of questioning, I'd like us to further investigate whether the prince truly is above suspicion. We've just authorised him to leave the ship, at his own request, only a few days before this information came to light. The timing is a little too neat."

At this, the consul raised his hand. "If I may, captain?"

"You may not, and in this courtroom my title is Judge. Could you elaborate on why you don't suspect the prince, commander?"

"The prince worked the full shift. He did use the lavatory on two occasions, but I doubt he could have programmed a deep-space message and then sent it in the time he was gone."

"Could he have programmed a delayed message?" the captain asked. "Perhaps he told his console to dispatch it in a few hours?"

Plessis turned to Lieutenant Mith. "What are your thoughts, as our resident analyst?"

Mith made a face while she thought, and the room was focused on her. "I doubt it," she said at last. "There's a few good indicators if something like that had been programmed into the message. I didn't notice anything unusual in its meta-data."

"Thank you, Lieutenant. So, we're left with a conundrum. A message was sent by the prince, who has an alibi, plus he doesn't seem suicidal enough to tell the enemy to come and kidnap him."

"Does anyone else have access to the prince's quarters?"

Captain Dav'i asked.

"Yes, Judge," Plessis replied.

"Can you please list those people?"

"Consul Barclay also has high priority access to the prince's quarters."

The Consul stood, enraged. "How preposterous! I've served the empire for my entire life! I've guarded the prince since he could talk!"

Plessis shrugged. "I haven't found a motive for you yet, Consul, but that doesn't mean I won't stop searching for one."

"Do the door records indicate the consul ever entering the prince's quarters after the prince wasn't there?"

Plessis shook her head. "No Judge, the records show that the consul was always present in the room when the prince was. However, Ms Xu, you often spend a lot of time unsupervised in the prince's quarters, do you not?"

"Yes, I do."

A few audience members snickered, and Harmony saw two senior ensigns exchanged knowing glances. The captain glanced at the officers, and the room was silent again.

"Ms Xu," Plessis began. "Have you ever used the prince's personal console before?"

Harmony stared straight ahead at Consul Barclay, hardly blinking. The consul looked away, uncomfortable.

"Yes," she replied. "Several times." She concentrated on holding herself erect, despite the proceedings.

"Ms Xu, I'll ask again differently," Plessis said, circling. "Did you knowingly send—or were you privy to the sending of—confidential information to our enemies?"

"Do you think I tried to hurt him?" Harmony said,

suddenly. The consul looked up at her sharply. She felt tears well up in her eyes.

Caught off-guard, Plessis looked at Captain Dav'i quizzically.

"Is that a confession of guilt?"

Dav'i frowned. "Ms Xu, please answer the inquisitor's questions clearly."

"I'm not the one you should worry about," Harmony said. "You'd better look more closely at that consul. The way he talks to the prince, and the sway he has over him: it's not healthy."

The consul's hands tightened, and then relaxed.

"Is that a formal accusation?" the captain asked.

"Not at all," Harmony said with a sad smile. "I doubt accusing a consul would amount to very much. It's just a warning."

"For your information Judge," Plessis said. "The consul has an alibi. A spacer saw him walking along the walkways outside the officer's mess.

A spacer stood and removed the cap he was wearing. He saluted with a toothy grin at Captain Dav'i. "I saw him floating around down there that morning Your Judgeness. I remember it distinctly, on account of how creepy it was: him slinking around down there."

"Thank you for your testimony," the captain replied. The spacer sat down again. "Very well. In the absence of a proper confession, and with somewhat circumstantial evidence, I've decided on a verdict. For the time being, unless further concrete evidence is produced to the contrary, Harmony Xu will be locked in the brig until we return to Mars."

He shrugged apologetically. "It's not my preference, but

my first priority is protecting the crew, even if we don't have the full story. On Mars you will undergo a formal trial to determine if you are guilty of treason. You will have access to a legal team then."

Harmony was calmly escorted from the room. When the door had closed behind her, Dav'i turned to Plessis. "Inquisitor, you will continue your investigation when able. I'm not convinced we've gotten to the bottom of this. Have another look over the comm logs, and triple check any surveillance or door logs that we have access to."

The captain saluted the senior officers, who saluted in return.

"Well, thank goodness that nastiness is behind us," the consul whispered to himself.

13

Tam heard Du Mon's scream through his helmet's speakers, and leapt high into the air above the arrays of electronics to spot the assailant, rifle drawn. He nearly scraped his head on the roof above, and landed atop a memory bank. Tam could see the twin yellow beams of a helmet's headlamps as they wavered across the prince's body. The headlamps suddenly switched off, and Du Mon's scream stopped abruptly.

"Oh," the prince said.

"I can't spot the hostile," Tam said. The barrel of his rifle strafed the darkness.

A diffuse blue light, from Du Mon's helmet, washed over the individual. From his perch, Tam could see make out the general shape of the assailant: Martian height. They wore a mining helmet: twin yellow headlamps on either side of the forehead, as opposed to the single blue lamp on the side of his own military suit.

"It's a friendly: Ceres miner. Switching to the general frequency." In the darkness of the data centre, the person helped the prince stand.

Tam exhaled, and relaxed his trigger finger. He changed the radio frequency to the unsecured general channel, and jumped softly from the memory bank, so that he was standing behind the miner.

"—think I would see help ever again," came the deep

baritone over the channel.

"Are you the only survivor?" Du Mon asked. There was authority in his voice, as his upbringing and training from the officer's academy kicked in.

"No sir," the miner replied. Tam heard him sniff. "There's a few families that I'm with."

"Are they somewhere safe? Can you take us to them?" Tam asked.

The miner looked around suddenly, searching. Du Mon pointed, and the miner turned and saw Tam, realising he was there for the first time. Du Mon's own lights, now switched on, created a reflective shine on the man's faceplate. Tam saw the hint of an unkempt brown beard.

"Yessir, I can take them to you. Oh um, take you to them," he replied eagerly, with a giggle. "I'll take you to them right now, we're all living in the—"

"—Stop," Tam commanded, and he trailed off. "I'm going to give you a password and a secure channel to talk on. Then, you can take us to the others."

He held up an arm, and the screen on his wrist showed the credentials. In the silence, while they waited for him to dial into the channel, it dawned on Tam that the miner had camouflaged his spacesuit. It was painted with caked, grey mud from Ceres' crust.

"I need you to answer some questions," Tam said into the military channel.

"Yes, yes. Please, can you turn off that headlamp?" he asked.

Du Mon switched it off, and they were suddenly standing in pitch darkness. There was an audible sigh from the miner.

"They'll see us with the light, so it's better if we just keep those lamps hidden, hmm, yes? This way."

The miner was only visible as a movement. He walked in a permanent stoop, his head whipping back and forth as they made their way deeper into the data centre. He awkwardly hefted a mining laser that had been cut away from its tripod.

"Wait," said Tam, as they scurried after him. "We need to know what we're dealing with. Are there any more survivors like you who might fire on us?"

"Oh yes, hmm." He stopped dead for a moment, and Du Mon nearly ran into him from behind. "No, I think it's just me out here. Sorry about shooting at you before, Mr–"

"–Xu," Du Mon lied. *No sense letting him know who I am.*

Tam looked at him with faint amusement.

"Mr Shoe" he said, with a thick, spacer accent. "I'm glad you two are here. With a troop of spacer marines here now, we might have a chance at fighting back."

"It's...no, never mind. We're here to collect information before our ship arrives."

The man nodded, and turned to keep walking.

"We aren't marines," Du Mon shouted. "Wait—"

Tam grabbed a hold of the man's shoulders firmly. He stopped. The memory banks surrounded them.

"What should we call you?" Du Mon asked.

"Milford. That's my family name, but most people use it."

"Mr Milford, you've mentioned a *them* and *fighting back*. You're saying that this destruction wasn't just a landquake? Some miscalculation from drilling too deep?"

The dark shape of Milford leaned in closely. "You mean you don't know Mr Shoe? I sent a distress beacon. It was very detailed."

"We didn't receive a detailed distress message," Tam

corrected. "Nor did our ship the *Socrates*, which is on its way here now. We only received the general panic alarm over radio."

There was a pause.

"There's only two of you?" he asked.

"That's correct. We need you to tell us what happened here, exactly?"

"I can't believe it," Milford said.

"I need you to believe it, and tell me if something has attacked this facility. Is there a hostile force still on Ceres?"

Milford swallowed thickly over the mic. "They're inside Ceres."

"Who are inside Ceres?"

"I don't know how to explain it," he said. "I don't trouble myself with them. I just go and find the food, that's my job."

"There are hostiles here in the facility?" Tam asked.

"Ah—" Milford made a choking sound. "I'll show you."

"No, you don't need to show us, I just need to you describe it for us. How many hostiles do you estimate there are? What do they look like? Earthen? The Earth-Lunar mining guild? Where are they located?"

"Pilot Sunter, they're everywhere. They're not human."

Tam flicked the mic to private. "There's a good chance he's the only survivor here, and he's delusional."

Du Mon clenched a fist to signal that he'd heard it. "Are you sure that they aren't human? They could be wearing an armour that you don't recognise, or using drones or machines that are new?"

"No, no, they're not Earthen or Martian or anything in-between."

A large tremor shook the room, larger than any of the

previous ones. The memory banks swayed and rocked precariously around them. Concrete dust fell as the concrete above them began to buckle. The quake finished abruptly.

"We need to evacuate as soon as possible," Tam said quickly, just to Du Mon.

"I see Mr Milford. You said these invaders are everywhere. Is there somewhere that they are congregating?"

"Did you not see the big hole?" he asked. "They've got this thing down there that they—" Milford stopped, turned and scurried away from them. "This way, hmm, quickly, quickly, quickly."

They turned in the direction that Milford had been looking, and saw a dull, luminous green substance begin to fill the room.

"Huh?" Du Mon managed to say. He felt a strong grip on his arm, as Tam dragged him away from the light that was filling the data warehouse.

"They're eating here now," Milford said in an unnecessary whisper. "There's not many places left that are safe." He led them through a service corridor, out the back of the enormous data centre.

They were deeper into the facility than Tam had ever been, and he quickly became disoriented by the twists and turns that Milford took. Underneath his feet, Tam could feel the metal tracks built for service trucks and other autonomous machinery, tucked neatly into grooves in the concrete floor.

Some of the hallways had collapsed into piles of rubble that they scrambled over blindly. Tam could make out dead service robots among the debris. Other corridors looked perfectly intact, but were now covered in the same green luminescent liquid that they had fled from.

On two occasions, Milford led them down a corridor that was cracked and buckling. Dust billowed from the cracks in the concrete as it sank slowly under its own mass.

As they passed another tunnel that was covered in strings of the substance, Tam couldn't help himself.

"What's the glowing goo?" he asked over the secure channel.

"Something that the little buggers leave behind while they're eating," Milford replied. "It does a great job of propping up the service tunnels and airways, hmm, its like some sort of reinforcing glue."

"What makes it?" Du Mon asked. "You said something about little...?"

"Ah, well there's one now, hmm, isn't there?" Milford said.

He'd stopped at a fork in the service tunnel. In the distant right-hand tunnel, amidst the faint glow, they could see a creature about two metres long. It undulated and bulged like a maggot as it crawled towards them slowly on rows of tiny stub legs. The "glue" as Milford called it, poured out from the creature's proboscis as it followed the metal tracks on the floor.

"They like metal," Milford explained. "They're scouring the facility for it, and digesting it."

Behind the first maggot, Tam could see others as they slid along the walls and roof of the corridor towards them, coating the walls in a similar substance.

"Okay," Tam said. "Sorry I asked."

"I don't think we've ever encountered a species like this

before," Du Mon reasoned. "Do they seem intelligent Milford?"

"Hmm?" The old man looked at him, illuminated in the distant glow of the maggots' slime. "Nah they're not that clever really."

"Well, there you go."

"It's the big ones you have to watch out for," Milford said.

In the far distance, behind the maggots, there was something different that caught Tam's eye. It was hunched over in the confines of the tunnel, like an adult inside a children's playground. It followed carefully after the maggots and watching them closely. It moved on its hands and feet, carrying several maggots on its belly. Each arm was three metres long.

This new creature plucked one of the maggots, which was suckling at its teat, and delicately placed it on the roof ahead. The maggot dutifully began painting the roof with its mucus.

There's no air down here, Tam realised suddenly. *Why aren't they breathing?* He looked into the creature's milky white eyes, luminous and unblinking. He saw the intelligence there, assessing them. Milford coughed, and Tam gladly followed him down the other tunnel, away from the spectacle. They fled deeper into the safety of the darkness.

14

The airlock pressurised. The interior lit green, and then hissed open. Du Mon stepped through the metal doorway, and into a squatter's cavern that the Ceres survivors had carved out.

"There's thirty-seven of us here," Milford said. He unfastened his helmet, and started scratching a spot on his neck. Du Mon and Tam unfastened their own helmets with relief, and looked around at the survivors gathered there.

A sea of dirty, exhausted faces stared back at them in confusion. Then, they were suddenly rushed upon by the crowd. Old men shook Du Mon's hand rigorously, while a few children clung to his legs and squealed in delight. A young man resolutely pounded Tam on the back to welcome him. They were suddenly surrounded by new faces all talking at once.

"New friends!" yelled a young girl, barely three years old, above the din of people.

A handful of adults stood back from the others, watching Tam and Du Mon as they were rushed with introductions. One of the more reserved adults, a thin young mother who sat on an oil barrel breastfeeding, watched Du Mon carefully. She spoke softly to a hunchbacked old man, her mouth barely moving. Her bare breasts were smeared in mud.

Everyone was filthy. The youngest children ran about

naked. The three- or four-year-olds had mud caked thickly up to their elbows and across their bodies. Du Mon looked down, and saw that the concrete ground was damp. The airlock hissed closed behind him.

They were both quickly ushered deeper into the survivor's burrow underground. The prince was told to sit down on a metal drum that was turned sideways. Many other metal drums were placed around a temperature control unit that hummed loudly. The children's hammocks had been slung between the massive, mobile oxygen processors. It was unbearably hot.

Can people live in such conditions?

The oxygen was being cleaned, but the heat from the machines wasn't being adequately cooled by the temperature unit. Judging by the twisted metal around its outside, the unit had been pulled from somewhere else in the facility, and carried here to try and alleviate the heat.

Du Mon was handed a canteen of water by a stout, middle-aged woman. He took a sip, and nearly choked on the taste of dirt.

"That's all we've got, sorry hun."

"That's perfect, I was working up a thirst, thank you." Du Mon gagged quietly, and swallowed something solid.

"How long have you all been down here?" Tam asked the lady.

"Oh, perhaps several days? I'm not quite sure."

"It's probably closer to a week," Milford chimed in. "We've been dragging what we can down here, away from the hole that they're drilling."

"Why are there so few of you left?" Du Mon asked. "If you'll pardon the question," he quickly added.

"I was underground when it all happened," Milford replied. "The old fellow Rodney was working on the surface."

Milford gestured to the hunchbacked man, who begrudgingly joined them around the temperature unit. The younger children were sat inside the ring of drums and barrels, watching Du Mon and Tam wide-eyed. The other adults gathered around to listen.

"Can you tell us what you saw?" Tam asked. "Anything that you can remember might be useful."

The old man sighed. He looked at the young lady breastfeeding, and then back to Tam. "I didn't see what it was, not clearly, but I saw what it did."

"Just start with that," Du Mon said with a smile, he placed his hand on his forearm. *Reminds me of my own grandfather, just before he abdicated.*

"A siren went out, telling us to get underground to the shelters. I was far away from the facility, running cabling out to a new early-detection radar we were building south of here."

"We got the older folk doing some of the less strenuous work. It's part of the Emperor's compromise to a pension," Milford added.

The old man spat. "Wasn't any easier than digging, boy. Don't listen to what they feed you. I heard the siren for an attack come through my suit's radio. Left the radar out there, jumped in the truck, and booked it back to this facility."

"Did you see what caused the hole in the surface?"

"Wasn't a weapon or anything. It was a big worm. Biggest worm I've ever seen. It came shooting through space, but it somehow slowed itself down right at the end. Practically kissed Ceres with how smooth the landing was. Never seen anything move so easily through space. It grabbed hold of the surface about fifty kilometres from here." The old man stopped and breathed in a deep, ineffective breath.

"What happened after that?" Du Mon asked, and gave his arm a squeeze.

"Well, then it started thrashing around like something possessed, burrowing down. That caused the dust storm. Covered up everything. A big plume of Ceres was kicked up and out. Looked like the planetoid was bleeding. It kept spinning down, which was when the tremors started." He stopped, winced, and threw a thumb in the direction of the children listening. He lowered his voice to a hum. "The tremors and heat from its drilling caused the surface ice to melt under lots of folk. Then the surface froze again a moment later, after they'd sunk into it."

Tam gulped his water loudly. "So, under the surface there's…"

"Lots of bodies. We had to switch off the radio waves. Couldn't bear to hear them begging for rescue."

"Where's the worm now?" Tam asked. Du Mon could see his face was pale. They both knew the answer.

"It's burrowing through Ceres as we speak," he whispered. "Throwing the whole planet off-course. It'll hollow us out before long."

"How big is it?" Tam asked. "We couldn't see it from orbit."

The old man coughed, and it sounded wet. "I dunno. Six kilometres wide? Thirty kilometres long? Bigger than anything has any right to be."

Another tremor shook Ceres. The temperature regulator bounced across the floor. The shock lasted for two whole minutes. Dust showered down on them. The adults looked at the airlock with worried expressions. Milford ran back through the deluge of dust with a tube of quick-cement under his arm. Tam had lost the colour from his face, and Du Mon realised from the prickly sensation across his cheeks that he probably looked the same.

The shaking lessened again, and the group of survivors went back to their conversations. Beneath his feet, Du Mon could still feel the ground tremble softly, monotonously. A baby somewhere started crying, and a young man laughed with nervous energy.

"Well, now you probably understand our predicament," the old man said.

"Sir," Tam said. "We'll need to get all of you out of here as soon as possible. I doubt this will keep you safe for much longer. If what you've said is true, the worm is going to—"

"—Hello Sally!" the old man said loudly. A young girl scrambled onto his lap. Her hair was a helmet of dirt and mud, piled high on her head.

"What's a worm?" She asked.

"It's a little animal that lives on Earth," the old man explained. "Lucky for you, they don't like eating little girls named Sally!"

The girl squealed as he tickled her, and then she ran off with a light smack on her behind to encourage her. The old man wiped his eyes.

"That's my granddaughter," he said. "And my daughter's over there with my new grandson."

"I'll get you out of here," Du Mon said. "I promise you."

Milford sat down next to them and started stripping off his suit.

"How many spacesuits have you got?" Tam asked.

The old man smiled weakly. "One. One working spacesuit, and a lot of salvaged parts from the others that we used to repair it." The old man pointed down into the darkness, opposite the airlock. "These are the emergency bunkers, or what's left of them. There was a cave-in shortly after we all crawled down here." He coughed again. A thick, wet cough that lasted for an agonisingly long time.

"Are you okay?" Du Mon asked. The stout lady arrived with water and gave it to the old man.

"The water lines are leaking in here slowly," Milford explained. "We're filtering it as best we can. As long as we have enough food, we can keep feeding the water to the oxygen scrubbers, and trying to filter it for drinking."

The oxygen scrubbers were being manned by several spacers, working in shifts to manually crank the bellows pump. The new air wheezed slowly into the cavern.

Du Mon put his lips to the canteen of water again, and then stopped. "This water is bad," he said. "It's killing you. I feel terrible already, and I just had a sip."

"Yeah, it goes down the wrong way every time," the old man said.

Du Mon and Tam stood, excused themselves politely, and walked away from the group. Tam's brow was caked with grey dust. The sweat from his face had highlighted the furrow between his eyes.

"We can't get these people out of here," Du Mon said. "What did I just promise him?"

"It's okay, Your Grace."

"I can't save them."

Tam clasped his hands on Du Mon's shoulders. "Neither

of us can do that just now. If we get back to the corvette, we can secure help from the *Socrates*. The captain will figure something out. He'll save these people."

Du Mon nodded. There was a fire in Tam's eyes. "We can bomb these aliens from space. Especially that big, ugly one in the hallway," he shivered. "That's gonna' haunt my dreams."

"You're not leaving, are you?" Milford said from behind him.

Du Mon turned, his smile already in place.

"Just for a short while Milford. We're going to rendezvous with our ship."

Milford shook his head, and a wild panic filled his face. A look of desperation. "No, no, I brought you here so you can stay."

"Stay calm Milford," Du Mon said quickly.

"We need you to stay here and help us," Milford continued. "You need to help me get the supplies so everyone can live."

He grabbed Du Mon by the collar, and pulled him close. The man's tongue sounded fat and lazy in his throat.

"Stop, Milford."

"Do you know how much pressure I'm under to make sure these people live?" His face was inches from Du Mon's. The prince tasted his saccharine-sweet breath. "Do you have any idea?" Milford's eyes were unfocused, rolling in their sockets listlessly: a man on the brink. Milford's shouts were now attracting the attention of the other survivors.

"You don't know what I'd do to protect these people!"

"We do," Tam said calmly, cutting through the tirade. His rifle was levelled at Milford. The old man near the temperature unit stood up, but Tam gestured for him to sit again. Somewhere in the dim burrow, a small child started crying.

"Don't trouble yourselves," Tam said. "We can show ourselves outside." He jerked his head towards the door, and Du Mon screwed his helmet on tightly. Milford backed away from the gun, but Tam mimicked a system-error noise in his throat.

"Woah there, friend," he said. "I think we might need a guide to get us back to the surface." He raised his voice to the group of survivors arrayed around them. "We're going to borrow Milford for a bit. If he behaves himself, we can give him some rations to bring back here for you all. But, if you misbehave Milford, well..."

Tam waggled his eyebrows at the man.

"I can always just make-do with a map, and one less bullet."

15

The *Socrates*'s fusion-powered engines fired in reverse, slowing the capital ship's trajectory. Ceres loomed through the bridge's display screens, crisply outlined.

"Status report, Lieutenant Mith?" Captain Dav'i asked.

"The corvette is docked with Ceres, it's currently facing us," she said. "Broadcasting a communication pack."

"Access it, and put the audio through."

There was a hiss of radio static, and then the voice of pilot Tam Sunter came through as faintly as a whisper in their ears.

"Captain, I'm afraid the situation here is far worse than we previously thought." The voice was interrupted by a burst of static, and then it resumed. The communication was being relayed from the pilot's spacesuit, via the corvette, to them. Dav'i listened carefully to the report about the remaining miners. He allowed his forehead to crease at the mention of aliens, and nodded when the communication terminated.

"He can't be serious," said a mystified Lieutenant Mith.

"I think he was serious," Plessis replied. "I doubt they would have attempted a jaunt down to the surface if they knew about it beforehand."

"What can we assume then?" Dav'i said, thinking aloud. He ran his fingers through his moustache to ease his racing mind. "There's some sort of hostile force down there. Alien, foreign, advanced: whichever way we want to label it, they're hostile and Sunter doesn't understand them." He stared at the gaping wound that had been gouged into the surface of Ceres. *I wonder if my cousins are okay.* Dav'i shook his head, and opened the ship-wide channel.

"Attention crew," he began. "Ahead of us is Ceres, a significant outpost for Mars as I'm sure you're aware. We can confirm that there has been an attack on the miners and inhabitants, and many have been killed. I have cousins, aunts, and uncles down there. I'm sure many of you have family down there as well. We don't know much about what has happened, but we do know one thing: the people responsible for this attack are still down there."

He breathed in deeply, and allowed his voice to betray the emotions he was feeling. "I doubt this will ease the worry some of you must be feeling for your loved ones. Rest assured, however, we are armed to the teeth, and you've proven that we can handle anything that the solar system throws at us. Prepare your battle stations!"

Captain Dav'i signed off from the comm, and the bridge officers erupted in applause. A senior ensign furiously wiped the tears that bubbled in his eyes. Dimi stood up from the helm facing him, and clapped his enormous hands together in an applause like thunder. Dav'i lifted a hand in acknowledgement, and then settled into giving orders.

"Commander Plessis, get me a firing solution on whatever comes out of that hole. Pilot Sunter mentioned a big worm, so we're going to skewer it from a distance if we can help it. Lieutenant Mith, prep the laser-teams for counter missiles or anything similar. Dimi, bring us into a wide orbit around Ceres."

Dav'i arched his back, trying to stretch it, and shuffled deeper into his command chair.

"Plessis, I want us to shoot into that hole with precision. Tell the tactical team that I want us to cause minimal surface damage. Our initial bombardment should only be three warheads, I don't want to risk the lives of any survivors by shooting everything we have right away. One initial bombardment, wait, and hopefully we can bait that thing out of there for the real engagement. I want two corps of spacer marines ready to go down there and mop up any hostiles, and to extract our miners."

The bridge officers saluted, and then set about their work in a flurry of activity. Dav'i cinched the straps of his netting tightly across his sternum.

16

Tchk'Klikkik was uncomfortable. The walls of the hole were cramped and dark. As the Elder Seeker, long and worm-like, ate below her, she longed to be beneath the distant, raw light of the stars once again.

Looking up from the bottom of the chasm that the Elder Seeker had chewed in this sphere, she saw an asteroid in the far distance: it was moving too erratically for her liking. Again, it changed direction suddenly as she watched, and began to move to the dark places. Since entering this system, there had been many examples of these strange phenomenon.

The Elder Seeker had awoken, tasting something in Tchk's skin. *Food* and *question* were the electric smells that pricked her skin, arcing across the Elder Seeker's glands as it writhed. Tchk stroked the delicate gland tissue that she sat upon, but the Elder Seeker didn't return to its slumber.

Tchk's broodbrother was climbing the Elder Seeker's red, armoured carapace. He reached her, and cleaned his dark blue mandibles with a long, articulate arm so that he would look presentable. His eyes were bright and alert: large white disks that constantly assessed Tchk. *He does not like seeing me this unhealthy.*

They were far beyond the star charts that her ancestors had carved into the crimson armour of the Elder Seeker.

You have not been eating well. Her brother's thoughts were evident by the ultra-violet lights that snaked across his skin. *You will starve yourself soon enough.* He reached down his throat, his mandibles nearly reaching the second elbow joint. He pulled and tugged, and removed the half-digested meat.

I am not a hatching, Tchk flashed in irritation. *Don't feed me like one.* The sight of the food, however, awoke something inside her gut that she hadn't felt in a week now. She took the meat and swallowed it whole. *We're lost.*

All the brood knows, he responded. *Things here are not correct. No sun system we have come to is so...* there was no word for flat. *This planet's heat is weak and sickly, almost...* there was no word for unnatural. *I found something down inside this sphere. Little things that move intelligently, but can't speak.*

Are they like us? Tchk asked, curiosity getting the better of her.

Not at all. He sat opposite her, and rubbed the carapace of the Elder Seeker while he thought. *They die once they leave their exoskeletons. It is strange. Some of them did not have exoskeletons, and were already dead when we reached them. There is now only one or two active ones left down there, scurrying about the place. Very easy to kill. I had to put a few down who were threatening the hatchlings.*

Could we breed them? Tchk thought through her skin.

Not enough meat. Something has dug burrows through this sphere, but it was not a seeker or its larvae. There are no new burrows either. Maybe ones like us dug here long ago?

Tchk stared down at the ancient language etched onto the Elder Seeker's flesh. *Have the larvae eaten enough?* She sent.

They need more time, her brother responded.

I need to investigate something amongst the many lights. Keep the larvae feeding until we return.

You don't want me to come with? The long, thick hair around his eyes vibrated.

I don't think so, Tchk cleaned her brother's face with a hand coated in her saliva. *Keep the brood working while we're gone. This shouldn't take long.*

Her brother began the long climb down from the Elder Seeker. He leapt easily to the cavern's wall, and collected his larvae from there. A particularly fat larvae was moving more slowly than the others. He hugged the wall of the cavern, and began to eat.

Move request, were the signals that Tchk'Klikkik carefully sent to the Elder Seeker. Their broodmother had taught her to control her skin's electric currents long ago. Now her broodmother was buried in the Elder Seeker's carapace, a few kilometres away. The Elder Seeker deigned to obey her, and began a rhythmic swirling motion, pushing itself out into the open space of many lights. Tchk carefully hooked her feet into the gland beneath her, as she began to float again.

Once her brood finished eating this sphere, they would travel further inward to the sun system. *There must be larger spheres further inward,* she thought. *Spheres that the Elder Seeker can properly eat, with a metal core.*

The Elder Seeker must have sensed the change in her mood. The glands beneath her hummed in contentment as the Elder Seeker pushed out further and further away. Through her excellent eyes, Tchk could see bright lights blink from the strange, symmetrical rock that was now orbiting the sphere. There were two smaller rocks with it. They were long, possibly oblong, and matching. Beneath her, the Elder Seeker sent the smell of confusion and hunger. *There are heat cores inside those rocks, just like a sphere.*

Confused, Tchk looked up at the many lights, and back at the retreating sphere that the Elder Seeker had burrowed into. Ahead, the mineral rock began accelerating away from them. Reluctant to let a potential meal leave, Tchk sent the pheromone that said *food* to the Elder Seeker, and a direction. The Elder Seeker began to undulate rhythmically beneath her as it swam through the great expanse of space. She felt the void upon her flesh, and felt comfortable once again.

17

It rose up through space, writhing through the void. It was alive, and it was impossible. The bridge had fallen silent when it appeared on the tactical sensors, registering as an asteroid due to its immense mass.

Dav'i punched the ship-wide comms. "The enemy will engage us in minutes. Battle stations."

"It isn't responding to our radio frequencies," Commander Plessis advised.

"Give me a tactical analysis when you can Plessis," Captain Dav'i said quietly. *Good luck with that*, he thought. "Tell the *Sullivan* and *Montessori* to withdraw as far as possible. Comms, I want you broadcasting everything we see and hear back to Mars. Live feed, as much as the computer can compress." The senior ensign beside him sat frozen, mouth agape. Dav'i leaned over and clicked his fingers in the young boy's face. "Oi."

The boy tore his attention away from the screen and looked wide-eyed at the captain.

"Live feed this to Mars," Dav'i repeated.

"Yessir," the young boy said. He began tapping the air above his console with trembling hands.

Dav'i looked around at the officers on the bridge in front of him: at the rows of men and women who watched him from their bays expectantly. Dav'i glanced at the screen again, and at the maw that was snaking towards them greedily. He hit the ship-wide comm again.

"This is the captain speaking. I know many of you may be afraid. The enemy's...transport...is unusual, and no doubt designed to inspire fear. This thing has dealt a serious blow to Martian mining operations out here. That means, for some of you, this enemy has the blood of friends and family on its...hands." He shook his head. "We're going to show it what happens when it attacks His Majesty's property."

He stood, to project his voice better. "We're going to prove to this enemy that Martians are no pushovers. We'll make them regret attacking our brothers and our aunts and our cousins! We'll show them what real pitched battle looks like!"

A hearty cheer rose up across the ship. The cheer on the bridge was still audible, but less enthusiastic. The bridge crew were still watching the worm as it kicked and squirmed and limped towards them.

Dav'i sat again in his command chair, and fastened his crash netting. He fastened the breathing tubes across his face, and then turned his attention to Plessis, who was making calculations across her console.

"Tactical analysis?" he asked.

"It's approximately six kilometres in diameter, and at least thirty-five in length. It's gargantuan sir. The sensors are having a hard time probing it. There's only a small amount of metal inside."

"A small amount of metal? So, what's it—" Dav'i saw the wide eyes of several bridge crew, and levelled his voice. He plastered on that easy and jolly smile that he'd honed for reassurance. "So that's it's game," he said much more loudly.

"Some sort of sensor scrambling."

The eyes turned back to their stations, but Dav'i kept the smile. Plessis lowered her voice conspiratorially. "It's not like anything else I've ever seen. I don't know how deep its armour goes."

"We can just pummel it and find out," he said.

"Depends on how effective our weapons are," Plessis responded simply. "More troubling is how its moving. We aren't detecting any signs of exhaust: no radiation, no ion trails, no smoke clouds."

"Not even a fart?"

"No sir."

"Do you have a lock with missiles?"

"Yes sir. The enemy has a good heat signature, and plenty of mass for the missiles to lock onto."

"Fire the tubes when ready, a conservative volley please."

The *Socrates*, rolling calmly and evenly in comparison to the worm's sporadic spasms and twitches, bore to the starboard. As it rolled, the first six missiles were launched. Their engines lit up the *Socrates* brilliantly, and then they were away, hurtling through the frictionless void towards the creature.

Moments before impact, the enemy twisted violently downwards, exposing its back to the missiles, which exploded as faint pinpricks of light against its dazzling, pale carapace. Its wriggling slowed for a moment, but then it continued onwards, undaunted.

"Damage estimate?" Dav'i asked.

"Minor sir," Plessis responded, her voice sounded far away. "I'd estimate it has at least a kilometre of armour. We sheared away nearly a hundred metres of red plating, and it continued onwards regardless."

"How long until it reaches us?"

"Calculating. Minutes sir, it's accelerating like we are, but it will easily intercept us at this rate."

Dav'i sat still, weighing up their options. *Are we better off trying to engage it with hit-and-run? That's only viable if this is its current top speed. We could try and slingshot around Ceres, but there could be debris that we're not aware of.*

"Fire two more conservative volleys, and target the same region," he instructed Plessis.

"I have a transmission from Ceres," a blonde ensign sang out. "It's Prince Du Mon and Pilot Sunter on the military channel, sir. They're making their way across the surface of Ceres and back to their corvette. Requesting additional orders."

"Tell them to rendezvous with the *Montessori*, and give the battle a wide berth," Dav'i replied.

"Missile volleys outbound," Plessis replied. "No sign of enemy retaliation just yet."

"Laserteams prepare for engagement," Dav'i commanded into his console. "Focus your fire on the same region as the missiles, we're going to peel back the layers of this thing. Nice and simple, by-the-book warfare."

Lights of acknowledgement lit up his face, and Dav'i readjusted himself in his crash netting.

"Missiles have contact," Plessis announced. "We've shaved off more armour. It's still coming."

"Helm, bring us about. I want you to try and fly under it so we can score the belly its protecting. Tactical, fire a heavy volley from our portside, so that we get kicked downwards.

Shoot the tubes cold, just rocket impulse."

"Aye sir," Dimi and Plessis replied in unison.

The *Socrates* changed direction suddenly, and the entire crew felt their weight increase sharply and uncomfortably, before lessening again. *What's the worm going to do?*

The enemy didn't register their change of direction as quickly as it should have. The *Socrates* shot half a kilometre beneath its underside, and Plessis shouted the firing command into the console.

Small spots of armour melted away from the underside of the creature, but not nearly enough. Plessis was cursing at the console and yelling instructions to the bay of tactical officers arrayed around her.

"—you call them out by name and tell them I will personally court-martial any lasermen who don't empty all of their energy at it."

"A problem, commander?" Captain Dav'i enquired.

"Many of the bays of lasermen aren't firing, now that they've got a visual feed of the enemy," she said. "They're frozen, and the team leaders are having to threaten them."

A very real fear gripped the captain's heart. *We might not make it. How long has it been since I've felt like this?* He looked down at the tactical officers, who begged the laser teams to shoot. The *Socrates* continued to ineffectively chip away at the underside of the creature.

"Tactical, tell them that if they don't fire, I'll blow them out of an airlock!" Dav'i yelled, his voice raised in a note of desperation that he didn't mean to convey. Spittle landed in a string across his orange moustache. "Tell them if they abandon their posts, I'll melt their skulls with their own lasers while they freeze in space!"

A proximity sensor screamed from the helm's console. "Brace for impact!" Dimi screamed.

A second later, there was a sickening sound of metal being torn. The ship had been hit, and the visual feed from outside spun chaotically. The internal gravity failed, and Dav'i blacked out for a moment as the *Socrates* spun tip-over-tail. He awoke to the warning sound of the emergency stability engines kicking in to correct their spin.

A carousel of red warnings lit up across the bridge, stating that the structural spine connecting the engines to the *Socrates* had broken off. They were engineless.

"Helm report," he said. His head felt sharp and heavy.

"It reacted to our movement captain, by swinging its tail to hit us. I didn't have enough time to correct our trajectory properly. We just clipped its tail."

From the sensors on his screen, Dav'i could see the red worm begin a large, arduous arc to follow them. The *Socrates* continued its trajectory, spinning end-over-end, on a heading out past Ceres.

It can take all the time it needs, Dav'i realised. *We aren't going anywhere.*

"Abandon ship."

"Sir?" Dimi turned around.

"Abandon ship."

Plessis was pale, staring at her console in disbelief. Her fingers shook. She keyed the evacuation codes, and then Dav'i pressed the confirmation. A klaxon sounded across the *Socrates*. The bridge's lights dimmed to a dark red warning that throbbed.

The bridge crew sat in stunned silence. A few began to hesitantly remove their crash netting.

"Evacuate now! That's an order!" Captain Dav'i yelled. It broke the spell. The senior ensigns and bridge officers began to hurriedly unfasten their netting. They jostled and kicked their way forward.

Dav'i saw the blonde ensign from the comms bay was struggling in the low gravity. Plessis unstrapped herself from her own webbing and braced herself against the console. She grabbed the ensign by her collar and belt, and hurled her towards the exit.

The senior ensign strapped into the comms station beside Dav'i hadn't moved. He produced a portable vac and began cleaning his console and crash netting thoroughly. Great droplets of sweat trailed the sides of his face. There was vapour suspended in the air around his face.

"What the Deimos are you doing?" Dav'i barked at him. "You heard the evacuation order." The senior ensign froze, looked at the captain, and back at his vac helplessly. He kept cleaning his station.

"Captain," Plessis said. "I'm going to ensure the bridge officers evacuate safely."

"Thank you," Dav'i said fondly. "I'll try and buy you some time." He glanced at the monitor. "We're passing by Ceres now," he said. "Plan four escape velocities away from the enemy, in a wide berth towards the *Sullivan* and *Montessori*, I'll notify them to receive you."

"Yessir," she said, but didn't move.

"I'll take a fighter and escape, once everyone is clear," he explained. "Don't wait for me, I'll be fine." Dav'i looked her firmly in the eye, and hoped that she'd believe it.

She kicked off towards the escape craft hanger. Dav'i watched her sail confidently through the bridge. She anchored, and hefted the senior ensign over her shoulder. He still clung to the vac as they floated away towards the escape craft.

Turning his attention back towards his console, Dav'i took a moment to remember the layout of the weapons system. *I've relied on Plessis for too long,* he thought glumly. *I always chewed out younger officers when they forgot the basics, but here I am.*

The sensors screamed a proximity alert. The sudden tone awoke a panic inside him, and he rifled through the settings clumsily. The fear was quickly dismissed, however, when he found Plessis' firing scheme: neatly labelled, and by-the-book.

Careful Plessis, I think I love you, he thought wistfully. The bulkheads and metal supports of the ship protested loudly as the missiles' engines kicked away from the *Socrates.* Brilliant pillars of light flashed across the maw and sides of the beast, and yet it kept coming.

He brought up the crew manifest on the bridge's large display screen. "First wave of crew away," he said to himself. Spacers, officers, and passengers were loaded into the escape craft: wafer-thin corvettes designed for speed and little else. As each cramped corvette was jettisoned from the wreckage of *Socrates,* a white flag appeared next to their names on the manifest.

The worm was nearly upon them again, and only two corvettes had launched. "Damn thing," Dav'i complained. He began digging through the console to find the laser subsystems, but suddenly the worm was atop them.

He couldn't remember how to slave the laser systems to his console, so Dav'i gave up and focussed his attention on the missiles instead. The worm's maw was open, ready to greedily envelope the *Socrates*. Desperately, he opened fire with every remaining missile. The *Socrates* kicked through space again, a torrent of anti-capital missiles accompanied by pitiful anti-fighter ones. Orange lights, warning him about the overheating tubes, lit up throughout the bridge.

Out in space, the missiles landed against the worm's maw and sides. They sheared layer upon layer of carapace armour away, and yet there was still more remaining.

The maw of the worm latched onto the *Socrates*, and the bulkhead above Dav'i screamed in protest. Then, the worm started thrashing. Dav'i glanced up at the crew manifest, *how many left?*

The lieutenant who used to cheat at cards had made it. The consul was away, on the first escape craft that had left. Even the possible traitor, Harmony Xu, had been dragged onto a transport by the ship's warden. Dimi had made it. The last transport launched, and sensors told him that it had immediately crashed into the grinding teeth of the worm.

There was a pain deep in his gut. *Wait, was Plessis on that one?* He searched the manifest, helpless now that the missiles were spent. Her name was naked, with no white flag attached. *She wasn't on it.* An image flashed through his mind: Plessis' body crushed underneath some machinery in a walkway, trodden by spacers fleeing to the escape craft. A fire burning up the oxygen around her while she bled—he pushed the image away.

The ship shook as the worm's mouth ground the *Socrates* to dust. He punched the console in frustration. Suddenly, a hand grasped his shoulder in an iron-grip. He flinched, as a lithe woman expertly slipped into the crash netting beside him. Dav'i whipped his around, and saw Plessis smiling at him smugly.

"You disobeyed me. You were given an order to evacuate," he said, but the accusation sounded weak.

"Just so we're clear for the future, sir," Plessis said calmly. "That was an order I was always going to disobey. You need to work on your people skills."

I thought I was going to die alone. He let out a hearty laugh. The emergency hatches behind them hissed shut to prevent pressure-loss to the bridge. The gas mask symbol flashed amber on his console, but he removed the mask instead. The bridge rocked and buckled in the mouth of the worm as it was ground down metre by metre. It was tossed around as easily as a fighter in atmosphere. The air around them grew suddenly chilly, and their breath froze in front of them.

Plessis was tapping furiously at her console, blindly sending out beams of lasers from whichever batteries were still working. She stopped and held her arms under her armpits suddenly. "I can't feel my fingers anymore," she said.

"You've done enough," Dav'i replied gently. He reached out his hand, and she let him take hers. They sat holding hands as the roof buckled lower and lower, gas screaming out of the gaps that appeared in the bulkhead above them.

"You could have evacuated too, you know," Plessis said.

"It's better this way," Dav'i said. "I don't think I could have ever retired anyway." He had started breathing rapidly, but couldn't quite get the air he needed. "Besides, I have a spotless record. I'd rather—" he gasped, "—people didn't read about me running from a worm."

"Not your fault. It was a big worm," Plessis gasped.

"You know," the captain wheezed. "I thought...if I was ever going to marry again..."

"Dav'i," she gasped quietly. "Don't spoil the moment."

The bulkhead gave its last moan, and suddenly they sat, staring at the stars and the jaws of the worm encircling them.

The air left his lungs suddenly and soundlessly, and Dav'i felt like he'd been punched in the gut. A black fog was creeping across the edges of his vision, but he could still see the terrifying, grinding maw of the worm that churned around them. The remaining walls and floor of the bridge disintegrated silently in the bright vacuum of space, as rows of sharp, jagged teeth ground tirelessly at the metal.

Dav'i looked over at Plessis one last time, but saw that she had already died. Her eyes weren't focused on the stars, however, or the maw of the worm.

She had died smiling at him.

18

Tam and Du Mon were climbing up to the corvette when the sun was extinguished. A long, black shadow fell across them, and the tower shook so violently that Tam was forced to cling to a ladder with the crook of his elbow. He checked his safety line, a piece of white elastic rope that connected his belt to one of the many vertical railings that ran parallel to the rungs of the service ladder. It was fastened securely.

He craned his neck and torso around to look, and saw the alien worm. It unwound itself like a spool of yarn, billowing out of the planetoid and eclipsing the sun. Countless armoured segments along its body flexed, outlined with stark white sunlight. Several landquakes split the surface of Ceres, triggered by the force of the worm's movement as it kicked and spasmed to get free. Tam looked up at the prince, who was clinging to a ladder rung above him with his entire body.

"It's..." Du Mon's voice was broken, unbelieving.

"Let's move," Tam said, but his arms had been shaken and jostled too much. It was agony trying to straighten them. Du Mon didn't move, however, and continued to watch the worm as it left the planetoid, snaking its way into space. Tam looked at his wrist-mounted computer, and punched in the command for the corvette to warm up its engines. He kept climbing.

As Tam reached the prince, he could feel the tower as it buckled forward beneath them. He reached up and tugged on Du Mon's belt buckle. "Move it."

"I can't unbend my arm," the prince complained.

"It's just shock, my arms hurt as well."

"No, I don't think it is."

Tam could feel his weight increasing as the tower fell in slow motion through the light gravity. If their corvette hit the surface, however, it would still crumble.

We'll be stranded here, he realised. *I'd rather die in a cockpit.*

Tightening his grasp on the prince's belt, Tam pulled sharply, trying to break Du Mon's hold on the rung. The prince screamed coldly, and nearly fell. Tam held onto his belt resolutely as the prince released the rung completely and began to drift away from the tower. The prince nursed his right arm as Ceres tried to pull him back down.

"What's wrong with you?" Tam shouted, but suddenly saw the way Du Mon's arm was hanging. The idiot had slipped his arm into the rung, up to his armpit, in order to hold on. The tower's shaking had broken it just below the shoulder, and Tam had just done more damage.

"Oh, sorry."

The crying stopped abruptly, as the prince passed out from the pain. The tower was now tipped at a 70-degree angle, and picking up speed. Tam reached up to take the next rung, and felt a tug on his belt. His safety harness had reached the end of the vertical rail, and needed to be swapped over to the next one about him.

"I need you to start climbing," Tam said yelled over the radio. "I mean, I'd love to be a hero here. Ha! They'll sing the ballad of *Tam Sunter, Piggybacker of Princes* in all the bars back on Mars. Du Mon? You awake? My body is just about ready to let go and kill us both."

He willed his shaking arm to hold onto the prince's belt for a moment longer. He was exhausted from climbing, even in the lighter gravity. Thankfully, the prince stirred below him.

"I'd prefer it if they didn't sing that song."

Tam made sure Du Mon had a good grasp of the ladder's rung with one hand, and then let go of him. He coughed, and forced himself onwards. The tower was tipping faster now, nearly at 60 degrees. He could see the top of the tower. A few more rungs. He looked down, and saw the prince making good progress upwards, despite his one arm. Nearly there. He released his safety line from the rail, and reached up to attach it to the next railing.

If he'd been looking at the tower, Tam would have seen elevator cables inside the tower were being pulled taut. Du Mon, on the other hand, was looking up at Tam and saw the cables snap. The elevator's counterweight, now free, fell down through the tower. It pulled the elevator upwards sharply, towards the centre of the tower, and suddenly the tower's centre of mass shifted.

The tower's other legs gave way, as Du Mon yelled a warning that was too late. The jolt surprised Tam.

He let go of the ladder.

There was a moment of terror, as his hands clenched instinctively for the ladder's rung that was no longer within reach. Then, he felt the gentle tug of Ceres as it invited him back down. He floundered for a moment as he spun head over heels, spiralling downward. Tam saw Du Mon's hand swing out towards him, and he grabbed it instinctively.

"Got you," Du Mon said through gritted teeth. He was huffing and panting, and a guttural moan resounded from deep in his belly as Tam pulled on the broken shoulder joint.

Tam steadied himself, reached over, and grabbed the same rung that Du Mon was hanging from.

"You okay?" he asked.

Through his helmet's visor, Tam could see Du Mon as he gave a weak smile. The prince's face was dripping in a cloud of sweat, and his pupils were large, nearly obscuring the iris.

"Let's go, just a little farther."

The climb became much easier as the tower continued to fall. At 50 degrees, the tower's middle began to buckle inwards from the strain: the top of the tower bending up towards space, while the lower portions continued to dive towards the surface.

Tam got to the top of the tower, and pulled the prince up by his good shoulder. They staggered through the umbilical tunnel together. Du Mon's good arm hugging Tam's neck for support.

Tam keyed the entrance code for the ship with a shaking hand, and then beat on the doors of the airlock in frustration while it took its time dedusting them.

The pilot unceremoniously dumped the prince into the co-pilot's chair, and fastened the crash netting for him. He opened the plastic casing for the emergency controls, and hit the umbilical release on the controls. There was a warning klaxon, and he hit it again.

The corvette detached as the tower raced towards the ground, breaking apart in pieces. Tam flopped into his chair and fired the engines up and away from Ceres. The corvette protested under the light atmosphere of the planet, but Tam held the stick firmly. They shot up and away from the tower, and into the relative safety of space.

Du Mon was fiddling with the radio controls.

"Stop it," Tam said. "I'll do that."

"*Socrates* left a transmission for us to rendezvous with the *Montessori*, and some general coordinates."

"Stop ignoring me. There's some morphine in the compartment beside you."

The prince strained to reach down and around his crash netting, to the first aid cabinet on his left. Tam sent out a signal in the *Montessori*'s direction. Out in the distance, he could see pinpoints of light explode brilliantly.

"Do you think we'll see them again?" The prince asked.

"Who?"

"Milford and the others."

"Sure we will. They aren't going anywhere, and I reckon I can see the *Socrates* pulling out the big guns over there."

The prince nodded, and took a deep sigh. "We didn't end up dropping those supplies we promised."

"Yeah, well, I doubt Milford stuck around once that worm thing appeared."

Tam unfastened his crash netting, and set the ship to auto-pilot out and away from the direction the worm had been heading in.

He undid the prince's crash netting and unfastened his suit's neck ring, rolling the fabric down to the prince's elbows. Tam looked closely at the prince's shoulder.

"Phew."

Tam pulled the cap off a syringe of morphine, and dug it into the prince's bicep.

"How bad are we talking?" Du Mon asked with a weak smile.

"You shoulder doesn't look too bad," Tam replied. "In fact, purple is my favourite colour."

19

The consul floated in the *Montessori's* cramped docking bay, wringing his hands. Nearly a hundred people drifted through the bay: all survivors from the *Socrates*. Officers bumped against spacers. People spoke in hushed, disbelieving tones. Blankets were being donated from the *Montessori's* crew, and several of the older spacers were being wrapped in them by the younger crew, and then stuck to the bulkhead with adhesive straps so they could sleep.

"Are they nearly docked?" Consul Barclay asked the docking engineer. The red-haired lady floated upside-down in front of him, examining the docking schedule on her roster.

"The prince is in the queue," she said. "We've got another five escape craft from the *Socrates* to process first."

"Isn't there any way you could bump them higher on the list?" He asked, leaning over her shoulder to examine the schedule. "These are mostly spacer rank-and-file. Surely a pilot and the Emperor's son warrant special treatment?"

The engineer gave him a calculated look, and then kicked away from the rung she was using to anchor herself.

"His Highness is in a military-grade corvette, complete with armour and weapons," she called over her shoulder. "Those *lesser* people you spoke of, are flying in glorified coffins with engines strapped to them. If they're hit by a stray piece of debris that the computer can't see coming, we'll lose twenty or thirty good people in a second."

"Be that as it may," the consul said, bumping into people as he followed her. "I think the crown would certainly appreciate it if you did allow His Grace to make it aboard sooner."

An alarm sounded at the starboard docking hatch, and the engineer hit the button to release the pressure seal. The smell of body sweat and old air wafted through the docking bay, adding to the stench that Barclay thought he'd acclimatised to.

"I happen to have served alongside the Emperor's eldest son, Ju Tin, back when he was doing his military service," the engineer said confidently. "I distinctly remember the Emperor's speech at the conclusion of that service. He praised his son for being a 'man of the people', for 'following protocol' and all that. So no, I doubt the Emperor will sing my praises from the Palace rooftops if I let his son skip the line. Does that line usually work with people?"

As the new spacers spilled into the docking bay, they received a weary cheer from the survivors already there. The engineer greeted the last lady who flew out of the hatch, her cousin. They laughed and embraced.

Consul Barclay left the docking bay fuming, and ascended along the main artery that ran through the middle of *Montessori*, towards the bridge. He'd served time on a similar frigate, back when he completed his mandatory five years.

The bridge telescoped open automatically to admit a lieutenant, but remained shut when he arrived. A manual override sat next to the bridge's door. Barclay pulled a small paper diary from inside his breast pocket. He flipped through the pages quickly, and found the override code.

The *Montessori*'s mining bridge resembled a scaled-down version of the *Socrates'* own: most of the seats were designated for communications and coordination, however. Only two seats were reserved for laser guidance and combat.

"Excuse me," said Barclay loudly, drifting onto the bridge. The captain of the *Montessori* was reclining in his command chair, being hand-fed jerky by the companion lady who floated above him.

"Oh, pardon me for interrupting Captain Soona."

The obese man shifted in his chair uncomfortably to locate the consul. A look of idiotic joy vanished from his face.

"Who are you?" he asked, waving a hand to dismiss the lady who hung above him. He turned to the lieutenant who had just entered. "Did you let him in?"

The lieutenant crossed her arms, and shot him a look of unrestrained disgust. The consul swam over to address Soona properly. He noticed dust across the surface of the captain's console.

"My apologies again, my name is Consul Barclay. Eternal Member of the Royal Council, and Tutor to His Majesty Prince Du Mon. Protector of the Red Soil," he waved a hand dismissively. "And so on, and so on."

With each new title, the captain tried and failed to correct his posture. He'd obviously been strapped into his crash netting while he was already reclining. He hastily unfastened it and threw a salute while trying to bow in his chair. "My apologies Consul, I wasn't expecting you."

"That's quite alright Captain Soona, my name must have simply slipped your mind from when you perused the

Socrates' manifest."

A look of fear flashed in the captain's eyes. He wiped his mouth. "Yes, it must have slipped my mind from...back then."

"I was wondering if you would allow me to send an urgent communication to the Admiral?" Barclay asked. "It wouldn't be a long message, and I'm sure the Emperor would be extremely grateful."

"Of course," the captain replied. He nodded furiously. "Please Consul, um, avail yourself of my console."

"Thank you," the consul said with what he hoped was a warm smile, and not a pitiful one. Soona moved awkwardly to the First Mate's chair. Barclay sat in the captain's chair, and immediately regretted it. The captain had been sweating heavily despite the climate control. He took a small wipe from a pocket inside his sleeve, and removed the dust from the console. Captain Soona graciously accepted the dirtied wipe.

"I'm afraid the process of sending radar communications escapes me," Barclay admitted. "Perhaps you could have someone from the comms team assist me?"

"Of course, absolutely," Soona gushed. He waved over the lieutenant, who floated warily beside the consul, and pulled up the correct program. The captain waited happily in the First Mate's chair, leaning over to see what message the consul was sending.

"Captain Soona, if I may," the consul suggested. "I have two special tasks for you. First, could you have a word to the engineer in charge of the docking bay? She decided to leave Prince Du Mon waiting outside in line."

The captain nodded energetically again. "Of course. I'll make sure his corvette is docked right away sir."

"The second task is that we had a traitor named Harmony Xu aboard the *Socrates*. I'd like you to lock her up somewhere where she won't do any harm. She's a companion lady, very short."

A wave of excitement washed across the captain's face for a moment, and he grinned eagerly. "Of course, Consul, I know just the place: the door to my quarters can be deadlocked."

"I don't mind where you lock her up," Barclay replied. "However, it's imperative that the prince doesn't have to face her."

Soona lumbered out of the chair. The bridge's doorway closed with the sound of scraping metal.

"Are you the First Mate?" Barclay asked the lieutenant.

"Yessir," she replied.

He typed his message to the admiral, detailing his version of events. The consul sat back and read the report. He nodded his thanks to the lieutenant.

"Could you send that for me? I'm afraid these consoles elude me."

20

When Du Mon and Tam boarded the *Montessori,* a tired cheer went up from Tam's fellow pilots. He was welcomed with hearty back slaps, and a long embrace from the pilot Jenna Whit.

Du Mon, on the other hand, was welcomed with a few polite smiles from the senior ensigns. Everyone was grieving the *Socrates* and those who had been lost. *I didn't get to report back to Captain Dav'i properly. I didn't show Commander Plessis I could do it.*

Tam situated himself in the middle of the docking bay, and was handed a liquified coffee sachet.

"Can we get you anything?" asked one of the younger pilots.

"Du Mon here needs medical attention," he said.

"The *Montessori*'s cook knows how to reset bones!" piped one of the frigate's spacers.

A few unconscious bodies were being ferried out of the docking bay, towards the barracks for treatment. The head nurse from the *Socrates* stood in the doorway examining the injured crew as they floated past.

"This one first," she called, gesturing to a spacer who had lost everything below the knees. Blood faintly speckled the mask and hairnet she wore.

"The arm's actually feeling a lot better," Du Mon said

quickly. He demonstrated a tiny range of movement, which generated tendrils of silver pain along his neck and down to his fingertips.

"Suit yourself, but the ship's cook is a genius," the spacer replied. He gave a crooked thumbs-up. "He reset my wrist, nearly good-as-new."

A general gloom returned to the docking bay as more wounded arrived from the *Socrates*. The injured floated, some called feebly for help. Others were silent, like corpses. Several lasermen from the *Socrates*, who had actually seen the worm, were unwell. They rested against walls and the roof, staring at the bulkheads in shock.

Du Mon silently drifted away, leaving Tam to recall their journey and discoveries on *Ceres* to a stoic audience. A docking worker floated past, and Du Mon asked to see the manifest.

Reading through the list of people who had made it, he saw that the *Socrates*' surgeon had boarded the *Sullivan* instead. Barclay was aboard as well, he shivered. There was a name that caught his attention half-way down: Harmony Xu. Du Mon realised that he hadn't thought about her since leaving the *Socrates*. It struck him as strange, *didn't I like her a lot before the mission? Why did she slip from my mind?* She was classified as a prisoner, instead of a companion.

"Excuse me," he asked the engineer on duty. "Where is this person? The prisoner?"

"No idea," she said, short and sharp. "The captain took her away somewhere. If you'll excuse me, Your Loftiness, I've got several escape craft full of starving and dehydrated crew to dock."

She pushed away, and he was alone again. He floated out

to the bridge, which opened when he pushed the intercom. Captain Soona was hovering inside, fidgeting.

"Welcome, Your Grace," he said.

Barclay was also there, surprisingly. "It's good to see you again, Your Highness." He held onto the captain's chair, and performed an intricate bow reserved for zero-gravity. When he rose, he noticed the way that the prince's arm hung at his side.

"You're injured?" he asked, concern etched on his face. The consul approached him to inspect the arm, but Du Mon held out a hand in protest.

"Yes, it's good to be back," Du Mon replied. "I do need a shower, however, and some rest. Probably a surgeon too, as soon as we rendezvous with the *Sullivan*. Most importantly: there are several families of survivors trapped under the surface of Ceres who need urgent rescue. I gave them my word."

"Yes, the survivors, of course." Barclay said, his brow furrowed deeply. "That must have been a very troubling sight to behold. I'm sure we can hear the full report from Pilot Tam Sunter, while you recuperate."

"Your Grace," Soona spoke with breathless excitement. "I would be honoured to show you to the showers. Oh, the spacer facilities are hardly befitting Your Highness, however. I would certainly love to recommend my quarters for you—" He stopped abruptly, and threw a nervous glance at Barclay, whose eyebrows were now perched impossibly high on his forehead. "My apologies, Your Grace, I just remembered that my quarters aren't at all suitable right now."

"That's quite alright," the prince said with a weary smile.

He rubbed his neck, which was raw from the ring of his spacesuit. "I probably just need to be alone for a while. I'm sure your quarters will be sufficient for rest, no need to act humble."

The captain began to stutter something, but was interrupted by the consul.

"I'm afraid I must insist you don't use the captain's quarters Your Majesty," Barclay said, resting a hand on Du Mon's good shoulder.

"You insist?" the prince asked.

"Yes, I must forbid it, for your own well-being."

"You *forbid* it, Consul?"

Barclay realised his slip, and removed his hand.

Captain Soona raised a hand. "Allow me to go ahead and prepare the room adequately for you, sir. My lieutenant could give you a fabulous tour of the bridge while I clean things up over there."

Du Mon smiled. "I've learned a great many things about myself while I was away, captain. For example, I now know exactly what I smell like after almost a week without a shower. I know exactly how much pain it takes for me to soil myself. The room will be fine, or is there another problem you'd like to discuss with me?"

"Of course, how improper of me," Barclay said, tight-mouthed. "I do hope you will attend tomorrow's lesson promptly Your Grace. We have a lot to catch up on."

"That really depends on how long you can restrain yourself from interrupting my rest," Du Mon replied bitterly.

The consul nodded. "Very well, Your Grace."

Captain Soona had handcuffed Harmony to his bunk. So,

when Du Mon stepped through the door, he found a very red-faced Harmony, trying to cut through her chain with a nail file.

The captain tried to float past the prince so he could explain himself. "My apologies, Your Grace, I'll just quickly remove the prisoner from these quarters."

"I'm curious, what crime did she commit?" the prince asked.

"They think I'm a mole," Harmony said, flicking her hair out of her face. "A message went out, giving away *Socrates'* coordinates to the Earth-Lunar mining guild. They're blaming me for it."

"The consul has been updating me on the issue, Your Grace," the round captain said from behind Du Mon. "The message was sent from your quarters while Harmony was inside. A court martial aboard the *Socrates* determined she should be tried for treason once we return to Mars."

He stuck his hand through the door to slide past the prince, but then retracted it when the prince didn't move to let him through. Instead, Du Mon punched the door's controls, and it closed behind him. He locked the door with his console's login.

"Pig!" Harmony yelled at the door. She pouted at Du Mon. "If I had a weapon, I could've taken him."

"I don't doubt that," the prince said. He started rifling through the captain's drawers and cupboards.

"The key's in the drawer, near your knee," Harmony said. "No, the other knee."

Du Mon found the key, and unlocked her handcuffs. She embraced him then, winding her arms around his neck and drawing his lips down to hers.

"I missed you," she said.

"Well, I'm back," he said.

"You smell terrible."

"Help me out of my uniform, I need to shower."

Harmony helped Du Mon gingerly peel his uniform off, and gasped when she saw his shoulder. "It's barely attached Du," she said. "I'll call a nurse."

"I don't particularly want to be butchered thank you," he said. "That surgeon on *Socrates*, he knew how to stitch someone up. Pass me that bourbon inside the cabinet. I'll wait for the royal physician"

He drank until the pain was a dull reminder, and climbed into the shower. It was difficult operating the wet vac with one hand. It squirmed through the air like an eel.

He emerged from the shower feeling like a new man. Harmony was going through the captain's drawers and cupboards. A male nurse stood patiently in the room.

"What did I say about getting help?" the prince complained.

"I didn't call for him," Harmony said. She found a golden necklace, and pocketed it.

The nurse spent a good hour fussing over Du Mon's shoulder, strapping it to his body.

"You should at the very least let the head nurse examine it," the man said. "You could lose the use of your shoulder, or worse, we may have to amputate if it goes septic."

"Captain Dav'i died in the line of duty," Du Mon said. "The very least I can do is wait until the dying are treated first."

The nurse tentatively prescribed a selection of painkillers before the prince sent him away. Harmony sat on the captain's bunk, humming happily to herself.

"You've changed. A few days ago, you would have been hollering for the best medical attention money could buy." She threw a look of mock terror. "What happened on Ceres? Did a parasite burrow inside you, and make you humble?"

"I still want the best attention money can buy. I'm just willing to wait for it." Du Mon chuckled when he saw her bulging pockets. "Did you ever rob me like that?"

"No stupid," she laughed lightly, patting her pockets. "This is my companion fee. I did just spend two hours tied to his bed. A working girl needs to charge extra for that sort of thing, it'll ruin my reputation."

She took his good hand, and played with the water blisters that the docking tower had given him.

"Can we talk straight for a second?" Du Mon asked. He reclined as best he could against the fibrous netting of the bunk. "It feels like forever since I've seen you."

"Well, you didn't say goodbye before you left," Harmony said with a pout. "I mean, I expected a note at the very least."

"I was probably just nervous."

"Maybe, but I've noticed a pattern Du. Over the past month, each time you've walked out of a lesson with your Consul, you've been colder and more distant with me. Something shifts. A week later, I feel like we're connecting again, and boom! You change again. What does the consul say about me in those lessons?"

"He doesn't say anything about you at all. We talk about history and politics mostly."

"I think you're lying," she said, with a disdainful sniff. "Or very confused."

"Did you leak information about the *Socrates*?" he asked simply. "Did you want to sabotage the mission, or collaborate with Earthers?"

She shook her head and gently smiled at him. "No, and it doesn't even matter Du. Whether I did or I didn't, at least now we're actually talking. Now that I'm suspected of treason, you have to actually decide your future. No more empty promises about whisking me away and marrying me. No more weird limbo between our intimate moments."

Harmony tucked her knees under her chin, and wrapped her arms around her legs. She kept tipping sideways, and had to correct herself against the bulkhead every minute or so.

"For you to be labelled a convict on the register though," Du Mon shook his head. "You must have pleaded guilty."

"I did," she grinned widely. "And now you've got to make up your own mind, Your Highness. You can't keep Consul Barclay *and* me satisfied. You're going to have to choose.

"I wish you could see what I see: that your relationship with the consul is unhealthy Du Mon. He's manipulating you, and he probably always has. If you believe I'm innocent, and I hope you will, then that leaves the consul doesn't it? The only one with unfettered access to your quarters.

"He has motive, doesn't he? Neither of you have a stellar relationship with the other, and he probably resents being powerless out here: no administrators to boss around, no bows of respect. You could imagine a man like that trading away his charge for the wealth and power that the Earthers would offer him. A pile of yuan for you as a hostage, and another pile for all the secrets that he could divulge."

Du Mon laughed at that. "I don't think that's correct. Barclay values procedure and order more than anyone should. I doubt he'd throw himself into the grips of chaos for more recognition, it just isn't in his character."

"Well, you can believe me or believe him," she said. "Your choice, and whether it's right or wrong, you *are* going to have to choose. If you choose instead to sit back and let it play out: him versus me, then you'll lose all credibility in both our eyes. I reckon the consul wants you to cast me out yourself. That way it's your decision, and you won't resent him. I, on the other hand, want you to believe me when I say that I didn't do anything to hurt you."

There was a long pause, and Du Mon stood there, watching a fine strand of her hair as it drifted through the air. Harmony shrugged, and reclined against the netting as well.

"I can almost picture it," Du Mon said. "It's right there in front of me, you know?"

"What's that?"

"Me, leading a ship. Making decisions on the spot, everyone cheering. I can see it now: the five triangles of a captain, or the badge of parliamentary honour, or the crown of emperor."

"Which one is it then? Or does your decision-paralysis cover more than just matters of love?"

"It's all of them, Harmony. I want all of them, and at the same time I think they're all beneath me. As though I can do something better than all of them combined."

"You're confused Du."

"Of course I'm confused! Training my whole life in simulations and classrooms and under the wings of others, and I still have no idea what I'll do after my five-years' service is up." Du Mon counted his prospects off on his fingers. "I'll never see emperor. Not unless something terrible befalls the rest of my family. Secondly, I'd hate the responsibility of writing legislation, bringing it to my older brother, receiving his stamp of approval, sitting back down like a good younger brother ought to."

"So that just leaves captaincy."

"But I miss the luxuries of Mars. I want to be needed, but I don't want to make those snap decisions: to be a judge at a court martial, or to beat the ensigns who don't fall into line."

"It sounds like you want to be respected Du, just like all men. The problem is that you don't know how to obtain it."

"If I'd been born into a slightly better position, that choice would be much easier: I'd be Emperor if I was the eldest, or Warmaster if I was the second son. Or, if I'd been born into a lower station as the child of two spacers, then I wouldn't have as many paths to choose from. I'd have to work in space, or on an asteroid somewhere, and I'd probably be happier for it."

"That's true, perhaps you would," she reached over and drew a circle on his chest with her index finger. "It *has* been a while, you know."

Du Mon sighed, and kissed her on the forehead.

"What's that sigh for?" she asked.

"I think my mind works better when I'm alone," Du Mon said. "Maybe that's why I haven't been thinking well for most of my life. Excuse me."

He pushed away from the bunk, and floated to the captain's door. "You know my code, so you should probably lock this up behind me. That captain gives me the creeps."

Du Mon paused for a moment, staring at the door controls, and then exited.

21

Tam delivered his report while standing at-ease, feet anchored beneath a foothold. The *Montessori's* bridge didn't have an adjoining tactical room like the *Socrates* did, so Tam was forced to speak over the bustle of the bridge's operations.

Consul Barclay and Captain Soona examined the digital file on the captain's console, with Barclay occasionally asking Soona to navigate to a different part of the report. The captain happily obliged, tapping in the air with the intricate gestures required.

Like a parent reading to their child, Tam thought with amusement.

"I must thank you for such a detailed report, Pilot," Consul Barclay said.

"Very well-constructed, don't you think?" Soona added.

"Just to confirm something," the consul continued. "You only witnessed thirty-or-so survivors holed up in Ceres?"

"Our guide on Ceres, who incidentally turned hostile, mentioned there were thirty-seven survivors. I assume that includes himself."

"Thank you Pilot Sunter," said Captain Soona. The lieutenant on the bridge was waving for his attention. "Do you have any further questions Consul? No, um, well then, dismissed."

The pilot left, and was replaced by Soona's lieutenant, who had lost her chair to the consul.

"You have an update on the alien's position?" the consul asked.

"We've received a distress signal from the *Sullivan*," she said. Her normal, taciturn expression had been replaced with one of dread. "Shortly after devouring the *Socrates*, the enemy remained where it was for several hours, possibly repairing damage, who knows. Then it began to follow the *Sullivan*."

Captain Soona clasped a hand to his mouth. "You don't mean to say…"

"The *Sullivan* is putting up a good chase," she continued, "and the worm is ignoring all of the escape craft that the *Socrates* launched towards the *Sullivan*. They've all diverted course towards us."

"What's the status of the *Sullivan*?" Barclay asked brusquely.

"They're engaged with the enemy as we speak."

"Thank you, Lieutenant, um, please don't tell the others just yet will you?" Soona said, dismissing her. He waited until she was out-of-earshot, and then leaned in close to the consul. "We have to rescue the *Sullivan*, the rest of the *Socrates* crew, and those other poor souls on Ceres. I can't imagine how we'll do it, though."

Consul Barclay's face was stony, as he watched the telemetry data from the *Sullivan's* sensors begin painting the worm in glorious detail above the captain's console. The bridge's usual noise grew quiet, as they all stared at it in renewed horror.

It's somewhat beautiful, the consul thought. *An*

abomination, certainly, but you have to admire its singular dedication and drive. On the screen, escape craft began to peel away from the *Sullivan*, far fewer than the *Socrates* had available, and not enough to allow the survivors of *Socrates* and the crew of *Sullivan* to escape.

They must've drawn straws once the worm turned in their direction, Barclay guessed.

"Captain Soona," he began. "I don't want to overstep my authority here, but I'd like to make a suggestion for the benefit of His Majesty, the crew, and you."

"Please do," said Captain Soona, sweating profusely.

"Let's return to Mars. Leave the escape craft. Tell them to go and land on Ceres and pray. Leave the *Sullivan*. Leave Ceres to rot until reinforcements arrive." The consul wiped his nose. "If we stay out here, we're just delaying our certain death.

22

The tubes and arteries of the *Montessori* were quieter than he'd expected. With one arm, Du Mon huffed and pulled himself out of the main artery, where cargo and spacers flowed like a stream. He'd spent a few hours tucked away in the officer's mess, reviewing the raw data from the *Socrates'* battle with the worm. The data had cut off once the worm started chewing on the internal spine of the *Socrates*, which is when Du Mon decided he needed to do something else.

As he floated towards the armoury, the prince realised that he'd often seen Captain Dav'i wandering around the *Socrates* to inspect it before a battle. The captain was usually the last one on the bridge each morning as a result.

Is it the trait of a good captain, Du Mon thought, *to closely examine everything you are responsible for? Or is that just the trait of a good man?*

As he examined the *Montessori*'s armoury, he reflected on how unhappy he'd been with the captain when he first arrived. *I expected undivided attention from him*, Du Mon realised. *I was frustrated that he didn't instruct me like Barclay did.* It was the little habits that Dav'i had, which made the greatest impact.

The armoury was stocked well for a mining frigate, *but not well enough for a ship about to enter battle*. The quartermaster came floating over, protected by a ballistic plastic that separated them. He took Du Mon's requisition form for painkillers through a small window, and gave the prince a sympathetic smile.

"Sunter nearly pulled your arm off, did he?" he asked, floating to the back of the storeroom to retrieve the medicine.

"Yeah, just about," Du Mon said. "Not his fault though."

The prince looked around at the crates piled high. There were very few actual weapons in the armoury.

"How many missiles are we carrying?" Du Mon asked.

"I'd need the captain here before I told you that," he called back. "No offense, Your Grace."

Du Mon waved it off, and examined the equipment he could see strapped to the bulkhead, or arrayed neatly in racks. There were sonic charges for disintegrating rock, mining lasers for drilling hand-holds. There was even an ancient boring-drill for tunnelling through dirt or clay.

"Here ya go," said the quartermaster.

Du Mon dry swallowed the pills while the quartermaster watched, and then presented his tongue as evidence.

"I just thought what happened on Ceres, well, it was a mighty brave thing to do, Your Grace."

Du Mon smiled, thanked him, and began the slow descent through the *Montessori's* main artery, towards the docking bay. As he descended, an ensign grinned at him. Two spacers dodged around him expertly in zero gravity, and gave him some hearty pats on the back.

"Great work down there," one of them said.

It wasn't a big deal.

Du Mon found the source of the leak: Tam was telling his version of events down on Ceres.

"Nah, that's the end of the story. You don't want to hear what happened on the dreadful tower, do you?" Tam asked theatrically.

"Tell my brother what happened!" a spacer yelled.

Tam did, and with many adverbs that embellished things too much. *He can work a room just like Jason did. I wonder how many stories they swapped together.* When Lieutenant Mith caught sight of Du Mon, she pulled the prince into the middle of the crowd, who all began firing questions at him.

"Did the aliens hunt ya?" a one-eyed spacer asked.

"They didn't," Du Mon said. Then he added, "I would've left a trail of soft asteroids if they had."

"Who knew the prince had a funny-bone?" a burly woman said.

Is this why Ju Tin slept in the barracks? Du Mon wondered as the group guffawed. *It feels good.*

"The thing that floored me was the worm," Tam said, shaking his head.

A few lasermen nodded in solemn agreement. Another shivered.

"It shouldn't exist," Tam said, and swore quietly. "But there it was."

"Bigger than an asteroid," the shivering laserman agreed. "How do you fight an enemy the size of an asteroid?"

The question was interrupted by a ship-wide announcement for all crew to congregate in the docking bay. Another hundred bodies from the *Montessori*'s crew tumbled into the space, followed by Captain Soona, Consul Barclay, and a sour-faced lieutenant.

The docking bay was far too crowded. The usual cargo was now covered by spacers, who swarmed across the bulkheads. *Like ants.*

Captain Soona stepped forward, leaking sweat that hung in a cloud around him.

"As many of you have witnessed, or heard from those witnesses, we are currently fighting an enemy that we don't fully understand. Um, we aren't sure about what it is, or who's controlling it. We just received confirmation that the beast has attacked and destroyed the *Sullivan*. There are now three escape craft from the *Sullivan*, and two from the *Socrates*. We've instructed them to make Ceres orbit."

He breathed deeply in the stunned silence that followed, and glanced at the consul, who nodded solemnly. Soona looked at his tablet for a moment, gathering himself. Then he continued.

"I have decided, as captain, that the *Montessori* is unable to wage effective battle against what Pilot Sunter referred to as 'the worm' in his report."

"Why aren't they coming here to us?" asked a spacer with terrible burn scars across his neck and face. "How are we going to rescue them if they land on Ceres?"

"Speaking out of turn," the lieutenant said, reprimanding the spacer. She reminded Du Mon of a younger Commander Plessis.

"That's quite alright, Lieutenant," Soona replied. "I think everyone here is wondering the same thing. Ahem. The answer is that we will not be conducting any further rescue operations. We have already changed our course. We're flying back to Mars. The Admiral has already dispatched two capital ships, which will arrive in two days—"

Any further details that the captain might have been planning to add were quickly drowned in a cacophony of protests from spacers.

The lieutenant blew her whistle for silence, but the spacers continued to scream abuse down at the captain. The lieutenant blew the whistle again, but there was no lull in the noise. The consul shouted something in the lieutenant's ear. She frowned, and then exited the docking bay.

One of the older spacers called out. "Two days? Too long! They'll all be dead!" It was an oddly poetic phrase for a spacer, and the chant was taken up by others around him.

"They'll all be dead! They'll all be dead!"

"I'm not leaving my sister!" someone screamed.

The officers, floating in the middle of the docking bay, looked around with uncertainty as the walls swarmed and chanted.

"Calm down please, calm down everyone," the captain shouted nervously. The words were lost in the chanting.

The lieutenant returned with an officer's rifle from the quartermaster. The shouting died down at the sight of the weapon, and the red-faced woman who wielded it.

"What are you going to do?" a young spacer yelled. "Shoot us for wanting to save our friends and family?"

"That's exactly what we'll do," the consul said. He spoke in a long drawl that was somehow familiar to the prince, and the energy in the room began to wane.

"Your Grace, please come here," he gestured towards Du Mon, who felt his muscles obey lethargically.

The consul continued to address the room in a deep voice: a drone that reverberated across the room. His voice was a laser that pierced the will of every person.

"There are no bounds of authority, where the protection of the prince is at stake. I would do anything to protect him, even from himself, do you understand? If there is the slightest whiff of mutiny against the captain, I'll politely ask the lieutenant to put a hole through your head, the ship's ballistics rules be damned."

"What if I don't want to shoot anyone?" the lieutenant asked into the middle-distance ahead of her.

"You will," the consul said, his face strained. "Or you will hand me the weapon and I will carry out justice."

He turned to the room, and as the prince approached the consul, he could hear the guttural thrum of the old man's vocal cords. *What's happening? Why has everyone gone silent?*

"We will organise a hasty retreat, and further reinforcements. No sense losing any more lives or ships."

A drop of blood fell from the consul's nose, and a vein threatened to burst from his forehead. Tam looked like he might break free from the authority in the consul's voice, but then the consul locked eyes with him, and Tam lowered his gaze again. The consul's attention was fixed on the crowd, so he didn't notice the prince's eyes focusing through the haze that filled his brain.

The lieutenant had released her grip on the rifle with lazy fingers, and it floated across the docking bay towards the prince.

I've felt this before, the prince realised. *This helplessness.*

Du Mon reached out and plucked the rifle from in front of him. The consul stood, tall and gargantuan above him, so Du Mon simply continued to float past until he reached the docking bay door. He let his feet connect with the wall, and hooked his right foot under the guide rail that ran around the doorframe. He hung above the consul's head.

Du Mon held the rifle firmly in his good hand, around the barrel, and swung it as hard as he could, like a bat, into the back of the consul's neck. The swing felt slow in zero-g, and mid-swing the prince worried that it would merely bounce off the old man.

The rifle connected, however, and the consul's feet crumbled. His voice was suddenly cut off in a cry of anguish. Blood floated away from the consul's ear, like tiny red air bubbles. Du Mon let go of the weapon.

The spacers and officers snapped out of their trance. Captain Soona dabbed at his forehead furiously. His mouth flapped as he pointed an accusatory finger at Du Mon.

"What have you done?"

"Sorry," the prince said, his breathing was ragged. "If we run away now, I'll have broken a big promise I made, and I don't think I'd be able to live with myself after that. There's a lot of people counting on us. So, I figure we'll go kill a worm and save those escape craft, and those survivors on Ceres."

An eruption of celebration broke out across the ship, much to the captain's dismay, who was quick to point out the problem.

"Wait, this is mutiny!"

The word mutiny hung in the air.

"No," Du Mon corrected. "This is a change of leadership, and a long-overdue one, I'd gather. A mutiny is when someone who doesn't deserve authority takes it by force."

He looked up at the walls that swarmed with spacers. "It's funny actually, how little power a person truly has. It doesn't matter if you're a captain, prince, or an eternal member of the council. Those titles only matter if others are willing to obey you."

Captain Soona turned to the sour-faced lieutenant for support.

"Sweetheart, confine the prince to his quarters." He pointed to the door with a shaking hand, but the lieutenant grinned wickedly instead.

"I told you I hate that nickname," she said. "Go on, though. Plead your case to the rest of the crew, and see if they're willing to support you. Are you charismatic enough that these people would attack a prince if you commanded them to? Have you inspired such loyalty among your fellow compatriots that they will defend your dignity?"

Captain Soona looked around at the sea of faces. A companion woman gestured rudely at him. A young spacer rolled up her sleeves. Several of the men spat in disgust, their insults floating through the air towards him. Soona's posture visibly shrank.

"I thought not," she spat. "There's no dignity left to defend."

"You are excused, Mr Soona," the prince said. "The lieutenant will show you to a room where you won't be able to make trouble." The lieutenant nodded earnestly. Du Mon waved Soona away.

"If I were you, I'd hide there for the remainder of this voyage."

The consul floated, unconscious, in front of him.

"Can you treat him?" The prince asked the Head Nurse.

She nodded.

"When he comes to, gag him."

"With pleasure, Your Grace."

The docking bay was a buzz of anticipation. Tam floated over to him, and squeezed the prince's good shoulder. "We probably need a plan now."

Du Mon nodded, and called the cook over. Tam watched them converse for a moment. The cook saluted, and quickly exited the docking bay, with his assistants in tow.

"Captain Dav'i said to never fight on an empty stomach," Du Mon said, addressing the crew and survivors. "I'm going to honour that. We're going to break out the officer rations. You'll eat some meat, I'll make a plan, and then we'll go kill ourselves a worm."

An old spacer wept at the word *meat*.

Du Mon signalled the officers to join him, and they left the docking bay with the cheers of the spacers in their ears. Tam helped him along inside the artery, towards the bridge.

"Now we just need a plan," Tam said ruefully.

"Tam, there's something you should know about me," Du Mon said, as the ascended through the *Montessori*. "I've been raised by the consul to despise spontaneity. It's incredible that I even volunteered for the Ceres mission we went on."

"So, what are you saying?"

"I'm saying that I wouldn't have done anything in there if I didn't have a plan."

Tam saw the prince smiling smugly. "Then what was all that about them eating, while you made a plan?"

"I need volunteers to go and do something incredibly dangerous and stupid. If they're content, we'll get more volunteers."

"There's barely any armour on the *Montessori*, only enough to deflect debris. We have a few mining corvettes, and I'm pretty sure mining frigates only carry a small complement of missiles. How do you plan on killing something the size of an asteroid?"

"Well," the prince began. "We've already lived through the answer to *that* question."

23

Tam Sunter flicked off the flight-stabiliser. He sat, piloting the *Proctor*-class corvette he was now intimately familiar with. It banked slightly, as he adjusted their flightpath. Jenna was running a string of complaints beside him.

"It barely responds to the stick," she was saying. "Is there some sort of delay in the controls? A technical hiccup like that could get us killed, you know."

"We're packing a lot of mass," Tam said, and pointed to the other two corvettes on their port. "Those guys are handling just as poorly. Open a channel to *Socra*— sorry to *Montessori*."

Jenna did it, but blew a rude noise out of her mouth. "I don't want to die in a corvette Tam. My father would disown me at the funeral."

There was a burst of pink noise, and then the *Montessori* spoke.

"We're receiving you Squadron Leader," came the voice from tactical: Lieutenant Mith.

"Oh, um," he glanced at Jenna, wide-eyed, but she was already wiggling her eyebrows in his direction.

"Please repeat that Squadron Leader?"

Squadron Leader. Jace should be leading this mission.

"We're six minutes from engagement," Jenna chimed in, a little too cheerily. She hit the mute for a second. "Do you wish it was a different type of engagement?"

"Roger that, we're cheering you on," Mith's voice replied, innocently oblivious. There was a sound on the channel before it cut off, a chewing noise.

"You really don't find that lip-biting annoying?" Jenna asked.

"I find it cute and endearing," Tam replied gruffly. "You need to focus."

The *Montessori*'s bridge contained a mixed complement of officers from both the *Socrates* and *Montessori*, working in tandem to create a make-shift tactical bridge. Lieutenant Mith turned around and gave Du Mon a dazzling smile.

"The corvettes estimate three minutes until contact," she said.

"Thank you."

There was a painful silence after her report. The bridge officers, having received confirmations from their teams, now sat waiting. Some from the *Montessori* were fidgeting. A few of the *Socrates*' officers were staring at their consoles, white-knuckled.

Du Mon saw the *Montessori*'s lieutenant watching him steadily, awaiting orders.

"Lieutenant," he said. "I didn't catch your name."

"It's Plessis, Your Grace," she replied. The name stung a little, so he tried his best to smile.

"Any relation to Commander Plessis?"

She nodded. "My older sister. Pride of the family."

Du Mon heard no trace of jealousy in the statement. "How do you feel, having an older sibling who was so decorated?"

"Like I just said," a tear welled up in her eye, and hung

there resolutely. "I feel proud."

"You should," Du Mon said at last. "She respected me enough to correct me."

"Permission to correct you in the future, Acting-Captain Du Mon?" she asked. Her smile was her sister's.

"Granted," he glanced across at the small group of officers who sat waiting. "It's a bit depressing in here, don't you think?"

Lieutenant Mith laughed nervously, and then stood. "Captain, I was wondering if I might lead the crew in a song?"

"How enchanting." Du Mon pushed the ship-wide channel, and Mith sang the Martian anthem into her console with a shaking voice. She was quickly joined by Plessis, who was a confident contralto. Throughout the *Montessori*, a hundred voices joined in.

> *A young and ruddy nation,*
> *Barely generations old.*
> *We are the Martian people,*
> *With sweat, surpass our goals.*
>
> *We tamed a hostile planet,*
> *Each worth the might of ten,*
> *We are the race of Martians,*
> *No longer Earthen-bred.*
>
> *Yes, we are the Martian people,*
> *Fighting 'til the bitter end.*

24

The Elder Seeker chewed through the small, hot asteroids much faster than Tchk'Klikkik had anticipated. *Perhaps, they're hollow.* This system fascinated her, she realised, it was a feeling she hadn't experienced in a long time.

I was once so inquisitive, exploring the countless tombs and catacombs dug into the Elder Seeker. I'd explore every sphere while the Elder Seeker ate.

Her broodmother had carried the burden well, much better than Tchk did now. *I've lost something, without realising it. Maybe I'm just now finding it out here, in this strange system.*

Her eyes were able to pinpoint the last asteroid: no longer moving away, but remained stationary. She could see the heat that glowed inside it, and the beams of light that bounced between it and the three meteors that were flying towards her.

Should we chase down this last asteroid as well? Tchk wondered. She felt nervous from having spent so much time away from the other brood members. *They are probably worried.*

All her experience, and the stories from the brood, told her that there would be hotter, more mineral-rich spheres closer to the sun. *We could always hunt that asteroid later.* Tchk stopped that thought, however, with another. *It doesn't obey any law of movement I know.* A realisation struck her. *Perhaps the minerals here are reacting to the Elder Seeker? Are our movements somehow affecting these asteroids' orbits? Will it remain there?*

The three small meteors decelerated as they neared the Elder Seeker: heat erupting from one end. *Almost intelligent*, she thought. *Imagine that: a thinking rock, moving between stars like an Elder.* In each of the asteroids that the Elder had eaten, there had been a brood of the creatures inside. *Perhaps that's how they migrate between spheres*, she reasoned.

The Elder Seeker generated a slow and comfortable pulse of electricity from its glands as it finished its meal. Small flakes of debris, and many of those creatures, floated away from its maw. Many were curled into the shape of eggs. *Perhaps their shells were broken open while the Elder chewed.* The death of dumb creatures wasn't something she particularly relished in.

I think the Elder's had enough. She sent the command to *turn about*, which was when Tchk realised something was wrong.

25

The alien worm's exoskeleton reflected brilliantly in the sun's unceasing white light. *A beacon of blood and death ahead of us*, Tam thought gloomily. Beside him, Jenna keyed the military channel, and spoke calmly into her controls.

"Assault Groups, prepare for drop."

"Group One is ready," replied the spacer with the burnt face.

The other assault groups also sounded off their readiness. The corvettes flew around the cloud of debris that glistened from the worm's mouth: the remains of the *Sullivan*.

Then they were above the worm, flying along its spine like jets along a canyon. Tam gave the signal to decelerate, and the three corvettes, flying in formation, all fired their engines in reverse. They aimed for the blackened area of the worm's midsection, where the *Socrates'* missiles had peppered it.

"Doors opening in ten seconds," Jenna called, and set the door to open automatically. Their corvette had slowed to 350km per hour, then 250km, their bodies rapidly growing lighter. There was a pressure building in Tam's temples, which caused his eyes to bulge in protest. He felt dizzy and nauseous. Jenna made a burping sound.

They had slowed to a crawl, barely 30km per hour as the

worm began to shift and move, coming about. A klaxon sounded inside his helmet, and on the cargo camera feed, Tam saw the corvette's cargo door open. Thirty spacers, already fitted in their spacesuits, unstrapped themselves from the walls, roof, and floor of the cargo hold. From the three corvettes spilled nearly a frigate's worth of spacers.

They leapt in groups: five spacers, each carrying specialised mining equipment, all clung to a sixth one who was packing zero-g manoeuvring gear. As they fell towards the worm, the spacer with the zero-g gear slowed their descent.

Group One landed, and dug in their safety hooks: devices fastened to their safety tethers, that began drilling down into the worm's carapace automatically.

"This is Group One, we've landed."

"Any issues?" Jenna asked.

"Safety tethers are holding. A few broke their legs when they landed funny, but we'll carry them with us."

Tam hit the switch to close the cargo doors of the corvette. He punched the acceleration as the worm's tail began to sway and undulate, causing the worm to turn around. A collective *woah* went through the general channel, as the spacers clung to their safety lines.

One group of five spacers was bucked from the worm before they could attach their safety lines. They flew out into space, and a few seconds later, the spacer with zero-g gear was flying them back towards the worm again.

"They're a tenacious bunch, aren't they?" Jenna marvelled.

"Industrious too," Tam said as they flew out-of-range from the worm's writhing body. "Have a look at that."

Pinpoints of blue leapt out from the worm's armour, as the spacers began drilling additional safety tethers in a web-like pattern, securing their teams to the worm from several directions. As they worked, the spacers began singing a song about a young man who met a serpent at sea.

"So that's how it goes," Tam said. "I'd forgotten the opening stanza."

Now that they wouldn't float off the worm's back, the spacers began surveying the crater that they had landed on.

"Over here!" a spacer yelled into the channel. She was joined by several of the senior team members, who ran their instruments over the small indentation she'd found.

"Great work darling," the burnt spacer said. He placed a hand firmly on her helmet, and then announced it to the channel.

"There's less resistance at this spot. We'll coordinate over here."

They set about drilling a martian-sized hole in the worm's armour at that spot, straight down. Tam watched the worm begin to kick as the spacers drilled with precision. They superheated and carved away at the chitin in a circle, lifted ten or so layers of it, and then passed it to the surveyors behind them.

Tam gave the worm a wide berth, as it began to twitch and jerk its midsection at the site where they were drilling.

"Look at that," Jenna said in awe, as they circled beneath the creature. Along its underside, dug into the worm's very carapace, there were countless holes and burrows that wove, connected, and separated again in a latticework of chitin.

"Is that an injury? A parasite inside it?" Tam asked,

straining his neck to get a better look.

"Something can cut through it with ease," Jenna said, marvelling at the intricacies of how the worm had been eaten away. "Do those burrows look somewhat organised to you?"

On Mars, the colonists had discovered a particularly nasty parasite preserved in a frozen underground ocean. When they'd thawed it out, and carefully cloned it, researchers had found that it could easily burrow into a person's flesh, swimming and chewing through fat. It left attractive pock-mark holes just beneath the skin, which had led to it becoming a weight-loss fad for a few years.

Unlike the pock-marks from that parasite, however, these holes were organised and clustered together. A big chamber was surrounded by five or six smaller holes. A hundred metres away the pattern was repeated, albeit with slightly different-sized holes, or the arrangement being a few degrees off here and there.

"I reckon those aliens I saw down on Ceres live inside it," Tam said, horrified. "It's like a spaceship that you have to feed." He punched the radio to contact the *Montessori*, and relayed their sensor footage to the frigate.

"A living spaceship," Du Mon marvelled over the channel. "Could you imagine? If we could just grow spacecraft? That would put Mars a hundred, no, a thousand years ahead of Earth."

"Still have to feed it something," Tam reasoned. "And it looks like it'll gladly ingest entire planets before its satisfied. You'd probably have to eat through Mercury, Venus, and Earth to keep it alive."

"Tactical suggestion," Lieutenant Mith asked on the

bridge. "Shouldn't the spacer crews utilise those caverns that have already been dug, as a starting point, and drill down from there? It'd require a lot less digging from them."

"We'd lose our ability to survey the dig site," Lieutenant Plessis interjected. "I think it's more important to provide air support where possible, instead of saving digging time."

"It's a good suggestion Lieutenant Mith," Du Mon said. "But we've already invested time digging the safety tethers elsewhere."

There was a pause over the channel, and Tam banked to turn and fly past the worm again, which was now trying to turn and scrape its body with its mouth, like a leech exposed to salt. An image returned to Tam: *it's like someone desperately scraping ants away.*

"Assault Groups, status report?" Du Mon asked.

"The armour keeps growing back slowly," the burnt spacer reported. "Sneaky stuff."

Down on the worm, an old spacer was stood up to his waist in the hole they had dug, examining the layers and strata of armour.

"We'll be able to cut it a lot faster from this angle," the wizened spacer called into the channel. "Someone bring me those solar charges. Let's go down and then widen." He spoke with the calmness of a lecturer, standing in front of a theoretical puzzle.

They placed the charges, and then there was a flurry of activity as everyone scrambled away from the detonation site, digging new holes for safety lines as they went.

26

Tchk'Klikkik stopped trying to reason with the Elder Seeker. She had strained herself so much sending instructions of calm, that mucus now freely bled from her skin.

Fear. Pain. Dig. The signals that poured from the Elder were overwhelming. It wasn't listening to her anymore. Something was hurting it very precisely. Not a simple jab here or there from debris, but a concentrated attack.

Perhaps one of the other broods found us, the thought caused her to stand up on shaking legs. *They could be digging new burrows to supplant us.* She patted the gland beneath her with her foot, and then realised that she would have to go out and face whatever it was. *The Elder won't listen any longer, because I'm afraid as well.*

It was a terrible idea to venture out of the burrows between spheres. Most of her brood spent the time in forced hibernation, and she only allowed herself brief moments of lucidity to direct their movements. Stepping away from the gland, her feet found and adhered to the harshness of the Elder's red carapace.

She climbed up and out of the large chamber. It was a space that her ancestors had carefully excavated in order to commune with the Elder Seeker. She climbed out to the surface as quickly as she dared. Standing, exposed to the void, she looked out and over the Elder.

The asteroid that she had been watching carefully, was now circling around the Elder, and moving towards the sphere they had left.

A great beam of light and radiated heat suddenly burst halfway along the Elder Seeker's body, in an area that had not been lived on by her people yet. She hurried towards the source of the light.

27

The spacers regathered around the hole, and peered into it gingerly. The hole had widened slightly, but not nearly enough. The crater caused by the *Socrates'* missile bombardment was a hundred metres deep. The hole they had succeeded in drilling was only three metres or so deeper.

"I reckon," Group Two's leader suggested, "the reason we're having problems with this thing, is that this red stuff is too good at dissipating heat. Don't worry about those mining lasers anymore boys and girls," the wizened spacer shouted into the channel. "We'll use the manual tools to work it."

They'd barely begun digging, however, when a shout came along the channel from one of the corvettes.

"Hostile incoming," the man called desperately.

"Which direction?" the head spacer asked. The group of a hundred turned around desperately, looking for it.

"From the head-end, I'm flying over it now."

From the direction of the worm's head, the spacers saw a corvette shoot past in a blur. Behind it, scurrying quickly, was something that made several spacers release their bladders into their spacesuits.

In the clear expanse of space, it was visible for everyone. It cast a long, dark shadow ahead of it. Its face was coated in a milky substance, that didn't hide the hideous features beneath. Two eyes, large and bulbous atop its angular mandibles, saw them. It ran straight towards them on hands and backward-bent legs.

"Aim those mining lasers!" the old spacer yelled at the men and women near him. "Quickly people!"

Hearing the command, they scrambled to swivel the lasers on their tripods.

With the drilling into its nerve paused, the alien worm spotted Ceres, where it had been safe before. It began to move, desperately and recklessly flying in the direction of Ceres, and the *Montessori*.

Du Mon heard the report from Ceres. The *Sullivan*'s escape craft were being given the all-clear to evacuate."

"Did you find the survivors?" Du Mon asked through the channel.

"We did," came the distant voice of a *Sullivan* lieutenant, who was commanding one of the escape craft. "Are you clear to receive us?"

Du Mon looked back at the grotesque image of the worm, careening towards them. "How long until it reaches us?" he asked.

"Ten minutes," Lieutenant Plessis replied. "It's travelling faster than before."

"You're cleared for evacuation," Du Mon said to Ceres. "Just be quick about it."

Plessis hit the mute button, and sighed.

"This is a terrible idea, isn't it?" Du Mon asked, rubbing his forehead.

"Yessir," she replied. She cracked the knuckles on her right hand, one at a time. "But I doubt we'll get a second chance."

28

Tam saw the alien far too late as it scurried across the worm's carapace. A single target amidst a red desert.

"Why aren't these things fitted with missiles?" Jenna asked as he brought them lower, towards the worm. It had begun to move with purpose again, back towards Ceres.

It had reached Group Three, who were laying out support props and scaffolding when it reached them. The alien grabbed one of them, and simply tossed the spacer out into open space with disdain. The safety cable held them in place, so the alien snapped the cable in its mandibles.

Tam brought the corvette low. He tapped the controls with finesse, aiming to hit the alien's head with the bottom of the corvette. It would have worked too, if their shadow hadn't washed over the alien ahead of them, causing it to duck reflexively. They shot over it, and Tam had to pull away sharply to avoid crashing into the worm's body.

He punched corvette's bulkhead in frustration. "So close!"

Group Three were scrambling along the surface of the worm, hurrying towards the others in desperation. The alien reached out with long and graceful arms, each hand closing around the helmet of a spacer, and crushing it. Their deaths were accompanied by popping sounds on the radio channel, as the air rushed out of their helmets.

Group Two had the mining lasers ready, but couldn't fire into the whirlwind of spacers that leapt, ran, and floated limply away from the alien.

Tam circled back around, but could see that the alien was now tracking him.

Group One was waist-deep in the hole again. They slowly pried the chitin apart, cracking and splintering it with wedges and hammers. Someone had brought a pneumatic jack hammer, accompanied by another spacer who was hauling its generator towards the dig site with difficulty.

The alien crushed the torso of another spacer. Her screams gurgled in everyone's ears, until Lieutenant Mith gently lowered the volume from that spacer's helmet microphone.

"Five minutes remaining," Plessis announced to the bridge.

"How many escape craft haven't docked yet?" Du Mon asked via his console.

"Two sir," responded the engineer in the docking bay. "Waiting to our starboard. One is from *Socrates*, and they spent most of their fuel reserves. The other one is carrying the survivors from Ceres that you ordered to be rescued. That escape craft used up the remainder of its fuel breaking orbit. We'll have to bring them in manually while they drift."

"Orientate us for an escape velocity," Du Mon said to the helm.

"Sir, I don't think we can save everyone," Lieutenant Plessis said quietly in his ear. "We'll put everyone else in jeopardy."

Du Mon licked his teeth. "I think we can make it."

Plessis turned in her chair to him. Her jaw was locked

tightly, so that it didn't tremble. "We can't."

"Can we tow the two remaining escape craft that are dead in space?" Du Mon asked, signalling the docking bay engineer.

"We can probably tow one of them," the engineer said quickly. "The umbilical cord can only handle one."

On the sensors, Du Mon could see ten spacers traverse the distance between the *Montessori* and the two remaining escape craft, trailing the *Montessori*'s umbilical cord behind them.

As the worm accelerated, the spacers were finding it increasingly difficult to stand upright. It felt like a category five landquake. Safety tethers snapped as the plates across the worm's back moved together and apart, placing too much force on the taut cables. The shifting segments made aiming the laser turrets nearly impossible.

The dark alien crawled towards the spacers, seemingly unconcerned by the shifting movement of the worm.

A spacer was picked up by the alien, his legs crushed in its grasp. Held firmly in place for a moment, as the alien reached out to grab someone else, the spacer used the last of his strength to level his mining laser at the torso of the creature.

He fired.

The alien stopped, and its hand released him. It delicately touched the cauterised hole that now tunnelled through its spine, and then went limp.

The wizened spacer ran after the jackhammer as it bounced up into the air. It hung peaceful and suspended above him, while the worm buckled and writhed beneath him. He could see Ceres rapidly approach, as the worm swam furiously for its safety. The spacer leapt, and grabbed the jackhammer.

There were shouts across the open channel as the safety tethers continued to break. Several more people were thrown off and into the void. *Tam Sunter will have his work cut out for him*, the spacer thought. He attached the jackhammer to his belt, and continued to pull himself towards the hole they had burrowed, hand over hand.

I'm exhausted, he realised. *I haven't been this exhausted since...*

He heard more spacers scream as their hands or legs slipped, and they were suddenly tossed away into space, or left dangling helplessly as the worm dragged them all along.

He reached the hole with burning muscles, and arms that could barely move. *If I make it out of this alive, I'll be stuck in a movement chair for life.*

He angled the jackhammer down and into the softer layers of cartilage below.

"Time to eject," he called. He dug out another tether drill, and let it dig its way sideways into the hole he was cutting. He braced his legs on either side of the drill, with his back pressed painfully against the other wall of the hole. He unfastened the other safety lines that attached him to the others, and gave the command again.

"I'm detaching the tethers."

"What about the objective?" the burnt spacer called back.

"I've taken care of it," he lied, and hit the release command on his wrist computer.

Simultaneously, the web of safety tethers across the worm stiffened, and then released. A patchwork of cables, spacers, and heavy equipment bounced once against the worm's body, causing a cascade of screams, and then it was clear: floating away from Ceres at a new trajectory that the corvettes could intercept.

The jackhammer broke through the last layer of armour, and the old spacer stared at what he'd uncovered: it was a pillow of flesh that had a puckered opening at its centre. The spacer didn't recognise it as a gland, which was closely tied to the worm's nervous system.

He shrugged. "Looks important."

He put the jackhammer against the soft, spongy tissue. He began to drill through the nerve, and down into the worm's insides.

"Three minutes remaining," Plessis said quietly.

"Attach us to the escape craft that rescued the Ceres survivors," Du Mon said. The command felt bitter in his mouth. "Then tell your team to hold on, we're going to break orbit."

He watched the spacers receive their instructions. They looked around, uncertain, and then floated past the closer escape craft, to attach the umbilical tube to the escape craft carrying the Ceres survivors.

"The lieutenant in charge of the other escape craft would like to speak with you, sir," Lieutenant Mith said.

"Umbilical tube attached," Plessis said.

"Helm, take us away," the instruction felt like a failure.

The *Montessori* fired its engine out and away from Ceres, breaking orbit, and trailing a single escape craft behind it.

"Open the channel to the remaining escape craft," Du Mon said.

"Your Grace," came the strained voice of a lieutenant. "What's happening sir?"

"I'm so sorry," Du Mon replied. "We could only save one."

"I see," there were shouts of protest behind him. Someone screamed in protest. An ensign was sobbing.

The strained voice of the lieutenant broke over the top of the commotion. "No hard feelings sir. Civilians first, and all that."

"I'm sorry," Du Mon repeated, as the *Montessori* pulled away from Ceres.

"That's quite alright, sir." There was a pause.

"Can I address everyone on your craft?" Du Mon asked.

"What? Yes, um, of course."

I should say something special. Du Mon thought for a moment about the right words to say, but he never had a chance to say them.

When the worm was almost on top of Ceres, it jerked suddenly. It wiggled back and forth in blind agony, no longer able to concentrate on slowing. The worm careened past, obliterating the last escape craft. Du Mon felt the impact in his gut.

With its healthy momentum, the worm struck Ceres at speed, its head smashing into the mining facility, instead of neatly returning to the chasm it had dug.

The worm's elongated nervous system, which stretched along its entire length, was liquified by the impact. If the *Montessori* had been able to hear it, the sound would have been deafening. Ceres, now brittle from the great chasm that ran through its middle, broke into pieces.

29

By the time the Martian reinforcements arrived at Ceres, Du Mon's arm had turned black. A series of complex operations had been booked to try and save it.

When the prince exited the *Montessori*'s umbilical cord and stepped onto the capital ship *Plato*, he was surrounded by a whirlwind of cheering spacers and officers. The survivors from Ceres were quickly escorted to the medical bay by the *Plato*'s response team.

Du Mon nodded to Milford, who was wrapped in a blanket and drinking hot soup faster than the response team could ladle it out for him. Milford didn't notice him. The miner's eyes were closed in pure culinary ecstasy. The prince easily tore his eyes away from Milford, however, when he saw his father step forward.

"It's been a long time, son."

The emperor's hair and beard were painted gold, and his robes were a vibrant red. He embraced Du Mon, and gave a cursory glance at the prince's shoulder. The officers and spacers bowed low, before giving the imposing figure a wide berth.

In the corner of his eye, Du Mon saw Harmony dragged from the *Montessori* by its warden, down to the *Plato*'s brig. The emperor placed his hand on Du Mon's head in acknowledgement, and led him in the opposite direction.

"You seem troubled, Du," his father said, as they walked to the emperor's chambers. "Is the court martial troubling you? Consul Barclay will probably back down from it, if I ask him to."

"Let it go ahead," the prince replied, his mind distracted. "I want people to know I acted in the best interests of the crew."

"I doubt he'll want to instruct you any further," the emperor stroked his beard. "However, I'm sure I can find you a suitable replacement. There are a few consuls who have a more...flexible approach to instruction."

They entered the emperor's quarters, which were panelled with cedar, and trimmed in red and gold. They sat facing each other across the emperor's desk.

"Your first operation is scheduled for this afternoon," the emperor said. "Would you prefer it if they simply amputated your arm and fixed you up with something better?" The emperor gestured to his own arms. "Enhancements are quite useful in a pinch."

"I think it's a good reminder. I can live with any scars or problems that pop up later." Du Mon picked the lint off his shirt. "I do have two requests though, Your Grace."

"Please," the emperor gestured his consent.

"The first is about the remainder of my military service. I'd like to spend it investigating those creatures we fought. It's certainly possible that there's more out there."

"It does trouble me that we have a new enemy who could slip under our defences from outside the solar system."

The emperor frowned. He pulled two candies out from his desk and handed one to Du Mon. The Third Eternal Emperor of the Red Soil sucked noisily on his own candy.

"I'm worried, because we haven't worked out why they attacked Ceres," Du Mon said, wrapping and then unwrapping his candy, again and again.

"We will," the emperor said. "We've found what the scientists think is a breeding pair. Brought them in while they were clinging to a piece of Ceres, along with a bunch of those maggots and whatnot. The *Aristotle* has been tasked with staying out here and making sure we can bring them back to Mars safely, and without them dying on us."

"I'd like to study them. To try and communicate," Du Mon replied.

The emperor smiled warmly at his son. "It sounds like you have a career of science ahead of you."

"Maybe," the prince picked up a small ornament from his father's desk: a scale replica of the *Plato*. "Maybe one day we will even have a reason to go looking for more of them."

"Their technology alone is certainly appealing," the emperor replied. "You shouldn't worry about all this until after the trial finds you innocent, however." He gave a wink. "What was the last thing you wanted to ask?"

"How did you know that you loved mother?"

"Oh." The emperor thought for a moment, chewing. "There was an attempt on my life, five years before I took the throne. Don't look so surprised Du: it happens to every emperor. We just don't let anyone hear about it. Actually, I'm going to run Ju Tin's bodyguards through a drill in two weeks to see how they'd respond to a variety of attacks. Sorry, where was I?"

"Loving mother."

"Oh yes. It was an arranged marriage, just like yours will be, so I hadn't known her for very long. We were engaged at the time, and I'm significantly older, as you know, so I was certain that deep down she probably resented me a bit. We'd meet briefly, talk about how she was, discuss the wedding, and then we'd be chaperoned back to our respective houses.

"Well, it turned out that her second cousin was jealous of her approaching marriage to me, and took it upon himself to make sure the wedding never occurred. High treason, you understand, but not all that uncommon.

"Your mother heard about it. Her second cousin wasn't too subtle you see: roped in several unscrupulous people, and spent the night drinking and plotting with them. Your mother snuck away from her home in the middle of the night and announced herself at the palace, to warn me. Yes, terribly romantic isn't it? Also, completely improper and forbidden. Couldn't put the exact story in the theatre circuits as a result, unfortunately."

"So, my mother loved you enough to break the rules?"

"No, that's not what I'm saying at all," the emperor frowned. "She loved me enough to protect me, even from her own family. Even if, perhaps, the idea of marrying a stranger wasn't the most pleasant at the time. In return for that, I started loving her. It was a decision, you see. A conscious and ongoing one. Each day I choose to love your mother, and I hope that she will do the same."

"I need to talk to someone," Du Mon said, abruptly standing from his chair. "Thank you for the conversation, Your Grace."

"I'll see you at the memorial service."

30

Harmony tried to embrace Du Mon through the bars when she saw him enter the brig. The warden smacked her wrist.

"I'm sorry I wasn't there when you hit the consul," she said, rubbing her hand. "I would've paid good money to see that."

"He's recovering pretty well, thankfully," Du Mon said, and sat on the bench that faced her cell. The warden closed the brig's door, so they could have privacy.

"You seem unhappy Du," she said, and shrugged with her mouth. "Are you going to tell me what's wrong?"

"I know you sent those coordinates to the Earth-Lunar mining guild," Du Mon said quietly. "You set us up. All of us on the *Socrates*."

Harmony leaned on the plastic bars, confused. "I thought you realised it was the consul who did that," she said. "He also tried to take control of the entire *Montessori* by weaving some sort of psychiatric magic on everyone, in case you'd forgotten."

"He stepped way outside of his authority," Du Mon agreed evenly. "Even in the midst of that, however, he was adamant that he was protecting me. Both of you have justified yourselves with that claim. I've always resented him for babying me, for always being ready to catch me. It's misplaced, certainly."

"So why do you think it was me?" Harmony asked. She crossed her arms and blew a curl of hair out of her face. "And don't think I'm going to forgive you for accusing me about this. When we get back to Mars I might disappear, just to punish you."

"You had plenty of opportunities to send the message," Du Mon replied simply. "You even had my door code, which you could use to access my personal console."

"The consul could have also done that," Harmony said with a shrug.

"No, he couldn't have," Du Mon replied. "Because the consul is a fossil. He doesn't know how to use consoles properly, let alone send an encrypted message. He still uses a touch-operated tablet."

Harmony looked at her hands. "He could have made you send it, using his voice."

"Maybe," Du Mon said, but the word wasn't uncertain.

"You really believe it then," she said. "Why? What motive do you think I had?"

"I don't really know," Du Mon said. "Maybe you truly despise me, and hated spending time with me. Maybe sending those codes was a quick way for you to retire rich. I believe you when you say that you didn't want to hurt me. You probably just wanted to have me kidnapped instead, and returned peacefully to Mars."

Harmony looked up at him then, and magma boiled behind her eyes. "How dare you," she said. "How dare you think that I would do that to you."

"Then what's the story?" he asked.

Harmony remained expressionless for a long time, shaking her head. She turned and sat on her cell's bunk, watching him. She was silent for so long, that a small seed of doubt grew in his mind. *Maybe you miscalculated*, he thought.

"I love you," she said. "I wasn't lying when I said that. Do you remember what we fought about, before you went to Ceres?"

Du Mon wound his mind back. "You were angry, because I said I wanted to marry you."

"That's right. You'd said it over and over. I'd lost count. I started believing it too, until the consul noticed the way you looked at me. After those special lessons with him, you always treated me a little more coldly."

"You've always treated me that way as well, Harmony," Du Mon said, exasperated.

"I had to Du," she said, desperation filling her eyes. "Do you know how many times a man has promised me love, and I've traded that for extra favours? I *had* to put my guard up around you, because you were the first person who could afford to lift me out of my station in life. That's the problem though, your heritage is *too* perfect. You're royalty, and that's as good as a death sentence to my dreams of actually having you."

"So why contact pirates?" Du Mon asked.

"They weren't pirates," Harmony responded. "They were my father's employees."

Du Mon felt his heart stop. It reluctantly began ticking a second later.

"You're Earthen?" he asked.

"Half. My father is," she said. "Mum had a strange taste in men. Maybe I inherited that."

"So, you contacted your father?"

She nodded. "He's high up in the Earth-Lunar mining

guild. I told him I was finally willing to come and live with him, if I could bring you, plus two mining frigates and a capital ship worth of resources to help him disregard the risk."

Du Mon felt dizzy, and felt bile creeping up and over his tongue. "You wanted to kidnap me, and take me away to live on a mining frigate?"

"We'd have been together, Du," she said, and placed her hand on her heart. "I was willing to throw my future away for you, and I thought you were willing to do the same."

Maybe. Maybe I would have, if Jason hadn't died.

"I didn't expect Captain Dav'i to handle my father's preparations so well," she said with a shrug. "Luckily my father wasn't on those frigates, or I'd have been a lot more upset."

Du Mon shook his head in disbelief. "So, what was the plan then? Attack *Socrates*, and then what?"

"Once the *Socrates* was crippled, you and I would be taken back to the Earth-Lunar mining guild. They'd get to strip *Socrates* of its ablative armour, and it would have had to limp home, or wait for a rescue. Of course, that's not the way things panned out. I figured that if you no longer trusted the consul, I'd still had a chance of being with you and trying something else."

"You put my life in danger, and your life in danger as well," the prince could feel the anger bubble in his chest.

"It was worth the risk, Du."

He stood from the bench, and walked to the exit.

"Wait, are you really going to turn me in?" she asked. Fear had crept into her voice.

"I lost a friend in that raid you orchestrated," he said. Du

Mon's voice struggled to escape his throat. "I cried over Jason's body like a child, and in an hour, we're going to bury his ashes in space. But no, I'm not going to tell on you."

Relief flooded her face, but he held up his hand.

"Don't mistake my intent. I won't forgive you. You killed one of my few friends, at least indirectly. What we felt for each other these past months wasn't love. It was something else, something unhealthy. For all his faults, at least the consul wanted to protect me."

Harmony rushed to the bars and reached out between them, tears in her eyes.

"Du, don't do this."

"Please refer to me as Your Grace."

She withdrew her arms, and held them resolutely.

"I won't."

"I want you to understand that I have no more feelings for you, Ms Xu. None whatsoever. I'm going to let the courts decide how severe your treachery is, and I will testify to the consul's innocence. If they send you to a mining colony to work off your treason, I won't come rescue you. If your dad tries to bust you out, I'll personally hunt him down and drop a missile in his lap, cease-fire be damned. If the courts decide to shoot you, all the better."

She spat at him, and the ball of saliva landed between them.

"Don't be a coward," she said. "If you want me dead, you should just do it yourself. If you have to make your father do it, I'll know you still care for me."

"But that's precisely the point," Du Mon said with a smile. "If the court pardons you, then you can live your life content with the knowledge that I don't care if you live or die."

"Listen to yourself," she said. "You're not the man I fell in love with."

"I'm not," Du Mon agreed. "And that's a very good thing."

Epilogue

It had been five years since Prince Du Mon and Tam Sunter had finally sent Jason's ashes out into space to rest. As he drove across the red Martian desert with his friends, Du Mon finally worked up the courage to say it.

"I'm ready to see her, I think," Du Mon said to Tam, as the pilot drove them all to the research facility.

"Are you sure?" Tam asked, surprised. "You've refused all this time."

He nodded.

They approached the base of Mount Olympus. Tam activated a switch that was tucked under the controls. As the wheels of their rover churned up thick red clouds of dirt, Du Mon heard the acknowledgement ping.

The giant metal doors that were recessed against the base of Olympus opened, admitting them inside. They drove in silence through a service tunnel, until Plessis broke it.

"Do you regret spending so much time trying to communicate with the aliens?" she asked.

He thought for a moment. "It's a shame that we never learned to communicate with them well," he began. "There's possibly a whole slew of nuances we just didn't understand."

"They were also demoralised," Mith suggested. "At least, I guess that's what they were. You said they stopped eating?"

"Yeah. There's that," he sighed. "They were just a shell of

themselves by the time we managed to get them back here to Mars."

"Maybe you'll get another chance one day?" Mith's smile was contagious.

The transport broke free of the tunnel, and out into the research facility buried deep under Mars.

"I'm excited about your new project," Du Mon said.

"*Just* excited?" Plessis nearly choked. "You should be ecstatic for me!"

"Okay, I'm ecstatic then," he said, grinning.

They passed window after window of military secrets. The service tunnel suddenly opened up into an enormous underground hangar. Situated in the corner of it, along with several other prototypes, was the nose-cone of a capital ship.

Tam drove them up under it, and Du Mon leapt out of the rover as soon as he could. He stared up in awe at its immense size, and shuddered. It was a red carapace, coaxed into the shape of a Martian nose cone. Technicians were busily painting it in a fresh layer of mucus to halt its growth.

"It's like staring at that worm again," he said.

Plessis grabbed his bad hand in excitement and held it. It was the hand that always felt cold or hot or numb when the rest of him didn't.

"What do you think?" Plessis asked.

"We're going into deep space!" he shouted, startling the technicians.

"Do you feel better, now that you've seen her?" Plessis asked.

"Where's the rest of her though?" Du Mon asked, looking about the hangar.

"Well that's more confidential," she replied coyly. "But

let's just say that we're on track, and that this time next year we'll be hurtling out towards Pluto, and onwards."

"It's creepy to think of sleeping in those vats," Du Mon said with a shudder. "We could be asleep for a millennium before we find any other life out there."

"I think you'll make a dashing explorer," Mith said.

"What about your beloved husband?" Tam complained.

"You too, dear."

"Do you think you're ready to be a captain?" Plessis asked with a squeeze.

"I think so," Du Mon said. He looked at the three of them and smiled. "Because I know I'll have a good team."

About the Author

Jonathan E. Furneaux (pronounced: "fur-no"), is an author and educator who currently resides in Brisbane, Australia. In the second grade, his teacher let him write novels in the back of his mathematics exercise book instead of learning his times tables. As a result, he developed a joy of writing and literature, as well as an awkward pause before having to do any kind of counting.

Jonathan was awarded a High Commendation by the Fellowship of Australian Writers (QLD) for his first published short story: *The Second Father*.

Lessons from the Wreckage is his debut novel. He has also co-authored a non-fiction chapter in *The Contribution of Fiction to Organizational Ethics* (2014), where he argues that Star Trek can teach us how to run a business.

Visit **www.jonathanfurneaux.com** to discover his future projects (including some free stories), quickly find him on social media, or contact him with any questions or concerns you might have.